9

This Book Belongs to

. . . .

. . . .

. . . .

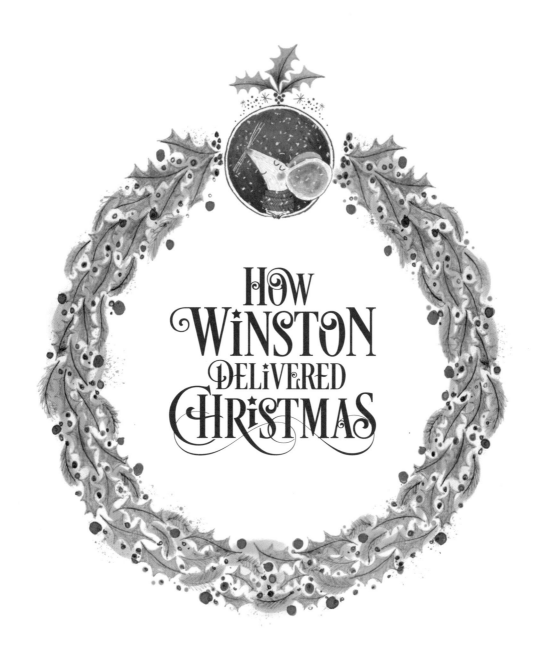

HOW WINSTON DELIVERED CHRISTMAS

Alex T. Smith

Silver Dolphin

Silver Dolphin Books

An imprint of Printers Row Publishing Group
A division of Readerlink Distribution Services, LLC
10350 Barnes Canyon Road, Suite 100, San Diego, CA 92121
www.silverdolphinbooks.com

Printers Row Publishing Group is a division of Readerlink Distribution
Services, LLC.
Silver Dolphin Books is a registered trademark of Readerlink Distribution
Services, LLC.

All notations of errors or omissions should be addressed to
Silver Dolphin Books, Editorial Department, at the above address.

ISBN: 978-1-68412-983-6

Manufactured, printed, and assembled in Heshan, China.
First printing, June 2019. LP/06/19
23 22 21 20 19   1 2 3 4 5

HOW TO READ THIS BOOK

ow Winston Delivered Christmas is a book written in 24 and a half chapters. You should start reading it on the December 1st, and then read one chapter a day until December 25th. The half chapter at the end is to be read on Christmas Day itself!

It could be fun to read the story with a grown-up, or even your whole family—get cozy and read a chapter together. Maybe have some Christmas cookies at the same time. Books and cookies go so nicely together, I think.

There are also lots of Christmassy activities to do. You don't have to do all of them if you don't want to and you don't have to do them on the day suggested. Do them whenever you have a few minutes and are feeling festive.

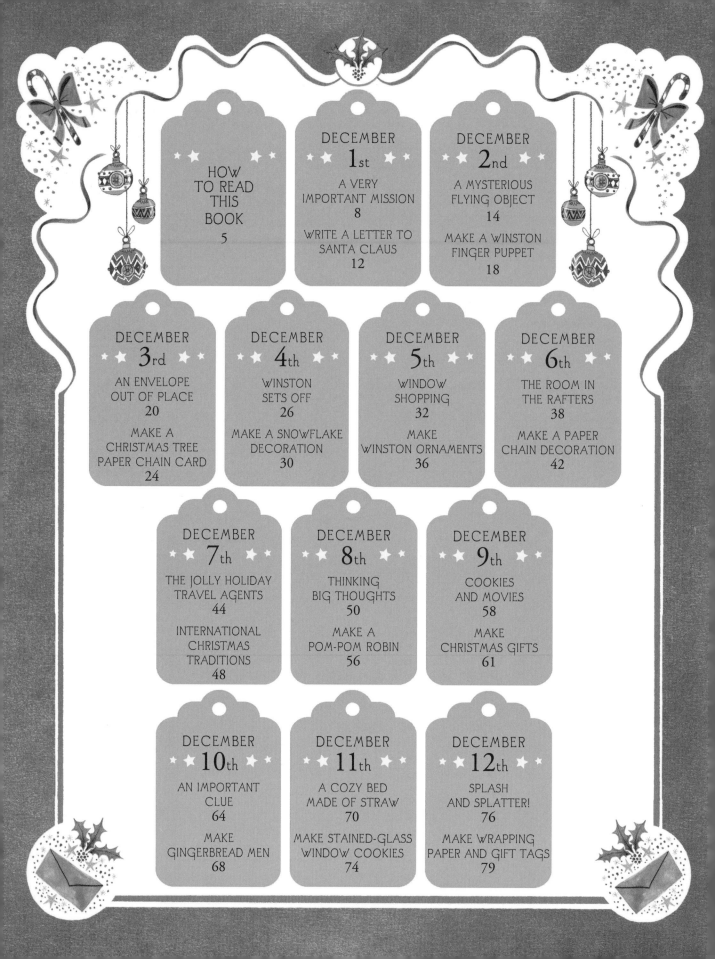

A VERY
IMPORTANT MISSION

The toy shop on Mistletoe Street was crowded and noisy.

There were exactly twelve minutes left before it was supposed to close for the holidays, but people were still shuffling in through the door hoping to pick up just one last present for a special someone, or to gaze at all the Christmas toys sitting on the shelves and admire the enormous doll's house in the window.

One person not looking at any of it was Oliver. His mom and dad owned the shop. He had been helping them all day—fetching and carrying and generally being very busy indeed. But now he quickly ducked out from under the counter where he'd been wrapping boxes. He flung his scarf around his neck and wiggled his way through the crowds and out into the busy street.

He was on a VERY important mission.

It was late afternoon, the moon was already up and snow had started to fall. Hundreds of snowflakes twirled through the air like ballerinas before landing daintily on the blanket of snow that had fallen over the past few days.

Oliver crunched down the street. He rushed past the bakery and the butcher's shop, sidestepped customers spilling out of the general store and the cheese shops, and swerved neatly around the ladies bustling out of the shop that sold fancy hats and ribbons. The entire night fizzed with Christmassy excitement.

On the corner of the street a brass band was standing in the cold, filling the evening air with a jazzy rendition of Oliver's favorite Christmas song. He stopped and listened for a moment before remembering his mission.

He weaved his way around the final knot of shoppers (their arms piled high with boxes and bags) and stopped in front of a bright red mailbox. He rummaged in his pockets.

They were full, as usual, with all the Extremely Important Things you need to have on your person when you are eight years old:

- A couple of paperclips (twisted open into wiggly strips of metal).
- Some string tangled up into several useless knots.
- The stub of a blunt pencil.
- And an old dry wrinkled chestnut collected in October.

All of this was Vital.

Eventually, Oliver found what he was actually looking for—an envelope. It wasn't too badly crumpled and he'd written the address on the front in his very best handwriting. He was a bit late in sending it, but he crossed his fingers and hoped it would get where it needed to go in time. He was just about to put it in the slot on the mailbox when someone called his name.

"Oliver! Oliver?"

It was his mom. She was standing in the doorway of their shop, waving at him. "Hurry up! I need your help wrapping these last few teddy bears!" she cried. "And it's much too cold to be outside without your coat on!"

"Coming!" called Oliver, waving back.

He quickly popped his letter in the box and scurried back down the street into the busy shop.

Now whether Oliver's envelope got caught up in the chilly breeze or was found by a shimmer of winter magic that was blowing that night nobody knows, but the letter didn't stay in the mailbox for long. When no one was looking, it slid back out and danced through the air and down the street, floating along between the snowflakes.

WRITE A LETTER TO SANTA CLAUS

Writing a letter to Santa Claus is the perfect way to kick off
the Christmas season! (Remember to mail it as soon as possible to
be sure it gets to the North Pole in time!)

YOU WILL NEED:

PAPER

PENS OR PENCILS

AN ENVELOPE

A STAMP

STICKERS OR ANY OTHER MATERIALS YOU HAVE FOR DECORATION

Santa Claus will really love seeing any drawings or decorations you add to your letter, and there are many ways you can make it special! Write your letter in the middle of the paper and draw pictures around what you have written. If you have stickers, you could use them to decorate the letter, too!

1. Start at the top right-hand corner of the page, and write "Dear Santa Claus."

2. It is a good idea to introduce yourself by telling Santa Claus your name, your age, and thanking him for any gifts you received last year. You can also tell him a joke if you know any good ones!

3. Now you can ask Santa Claus for anything you would like for Christmas this year.

4. Finish off your letter by sending your love to the reindeer and then sign your name at the bottom. Then you can decorate the letter.

5. Fold the letter in half and put it in your envelope. Write Santa Claus's address on the envelope: This is also Very Important.

> *Santa Claus*
> *Candy Cane Lane*
> *The North Pole HOHOHO*

6. Write your name and address at the top left of the envelope.

7. Finally, decorate your envelope with drawings and stickers, and seal it closed. Place a stamp on the envelope and mail the letter!

A MYSTERIOUS
FLYING OBJECT

A short while later, when the shops had all eventually closed, a small grubby white mouse poked his nose out from under the pile of garbage he had been rummaging in. He was in a dark alleyway, going through the trash cans trying to find something to eat and something he could wrap himself up in for the night, but he wasn't having much luck. Newspapers usually made good blankets, but all the pieces he could find tonight had been snowed on so were now soggy and not very cozy at all.

He looked around a bit more. *Oh! This looks better!* he thought. He'd found a piece of soft fabric poking out from under the snow. He gave it a good heave, but it turned out to be much smaller and not quite as stuck as he'd anticipated and he flew backward and landed on his bottom with a bump. He shook his ears and looked at the fabric. It wasn't large enough for him to use as a blanket. It was just a thin strip of tweed that had been thrown out by the man in the tailor shop nearby.

The little mouse sighed. "Never mind, Winston," he squeaked to himself. "You can use it as a scarf!" And he wrapped it around his neck.

Well, it certainly kept that little bit of him a touch warmer but it didn't do much for the rest of him. The night was bitterly cold and he was shivering from the top of his ears to the tip of his tail.

Winston decided to have a rest for a moment. When you are very tiny, rummaging through anything—especially human-sized trash cans—takes a lot of hard work. He found the driest corner of a cardboard box, settled himself down, and closed his eyes.

Winston took a big sniff. All around him, the evening air was filled with the smell of dinners being taken out of ovens and party food being laid out on silver trays in the houses and hotels nearby.

He sniffed again. He could smell roast potatoes and hams, fresh bread, and cheeses of all levels of delicious stinkiness.

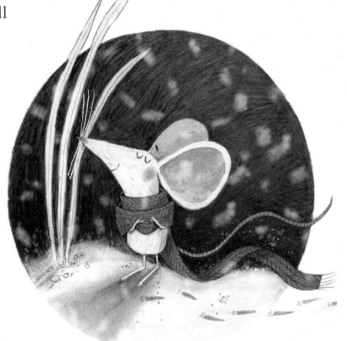

There was a little waft of eggnog in the air and a whiff of chocolate chip cookies so good that Winston wanted to roll himself up in it.

His stomach groaned and so did he. None of that food would find its way to his tummy. He needed to find something that he could nibble on now, and more importantly, somewhere warm and dry(ish) to sleep. But where? He'd looked everywhere in those trash cans and there was nothing useful or edible in any of them. He'd have to try elsewhere.

He stood up and shook the fresh snow from the top of his ears. He was just about to clamber down from his perch when he heard a whooshing sort of sound coming from behind him. He turned around to see what it was—probably a pigeon looking for something to eat too, he thought—but saw instead a flat, brownish object flying straight toward him! Before he could wiggle a whisker, the object crashed into him sending him flying through the air, and he landed head first in the freezing cold snow.

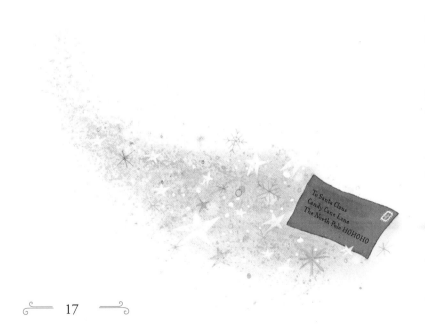

MAKE A WINSTON
FINGER PUPPET

Here's a way to make your very own little Winston!
You can stick him on your finger or pop him in your pocket
and take him anywhere you go!

YOU WILL NEED:
TWO SHEETS OF WHITE PAPER
SCISSORS
GLUE OR TAPE
PENCILS AND PENS
2-INCH PIECE OF STRING OR YARN

1. First of all, you need to create Winston's body. Find a medium-sized cereal bowl and place it on your paper. Take a pencil and draw a circle around the bowl and then carefully cut out the circle. Ask a grown-up to help you.

2. Now it's time to make Winston's ears. For these, find a bottle top, use it to draw two circles, and carefully cut them out. Fold both circles about a quarter of the way from the bottom. Now you have all the things you need to put Winston together!

3. Take the circle you have just made for Winston's body, make a single cut from the edge to the center, and roll it into a cone shape so that it is thin at the top but much wider at the bottom. Once you're happy with your cone put some tape down to hold it in place.

4. Put some glue on the bottom folds of the ears and stick them to Winston's body, roughly halfway down the cone.

5. Glue or tape the string or yarn to the body so that it dangles out of the end of the cone. But make sure you have put it on the same side as the ears!

6. Finally, find a black felt-tip pen and carefully draw on Winston's eyes. If you have a red or pink marker or crayon you could use that to draw his nose and maybe some nice rosy cheeks.

AN ENVELOPE
OUT OF PLACE

It took a few moments for Winston to turn himself up the right way and untangle his tail. He dusted himself off and rubbed his nose. *What just happened?* he wondered. What WAS that thing that had knocked him over?

He clambered back up the snow-covered pile of garbage and looked around to find who, or what, the culprit was. It didn't take him long to find it and his heart skipped a beat. It was an envelope. Winston couldn't believe his luck! Now for most, an ordinary envelope isn't something to get terribly excited about, but for Winston this was a real treat. Of all the things to find on a very cold winter's night like tonight an envelope—and a dryish one at that—was amazing! He'd be able to rip a little hole

in it and wiggle inside for the night. It would be like a nice papery sleeping bag that would keep him warm and snug and out of the wind and snow.

Winston sprang across the trash cans in several zingy leaps and picked it up. He was just about to tear a tiny hole in the side of it when something stopped him. He wasn't sure what it was, but something made his nose twitch and his whiskers tingle. He found himself turning the envelope around so he could read the writing on the front.

For a mouse, Winston was very good at reading. When your bed is usually made from bits of newspaper it's inevitable that you end up working out what all the black marks on the paper mean just to entertain yourself. Besides, getting a library card can be quite tricky when you are a mouse.

Winston ran his paw across the neat handwriting. It said:

To Santa Claus
Candy Cane Lane
The North Pole HOHOHO

URGENT!

He gasped.

This wasn't any ordinary envelope—it was addressed to Santa Claus! That must mean that the letter inside was very important. But what on earth was it doing floating about and knocking little mice off their feet? Surely it should be sitting in a neat pile in Santa Claus's warm, cozy workshop right now? *It must have got lost when the mailman was emptying the mailbox,* he thought. And as much as he really wanted to snuggle inside the envelope and get warm, he knew he couldn't possibly do that. This letter needed to get to Santa Claus!

"I'll take this to the mailbox and mail it so that it can get to the North Pole in time for Christmas Eve," Winston said to himself. But even as the words squeaked out of his mouth, he felt that something wasn't adding up. He counted the days off on his paws to try to work out what day, or rather—night, it actually was. When that didn't work (mice aren't great with numbers) he quickly rummaged through the garbage near him until he found the scrap of newspaper he'd uncovered earlier. It was from yesterday's edition—Winston knew that because he'd slept under another scrap of it the night before.

He turned it the right way up and unfolded the soggy corner. "Uh oh . . ." said Winston. The newspaper was dated December 23rd, which meant today was the 24th, and THAT meant that it was Christmas Eve!

MAKE A CHRISTMAS TREE PAPER CHAIN CARD

This is a very cool foldout card you can make to send to your favorite people. (Or keep it for yourself!)

YOU WILL NEED:

TWO PIECES OF GREEN PAPER

TAPE

SCISSORS

COLORED PENCILS

GOLD STAR STICKERS

1. Lay out two pieces of paper, and join them together with some tape.

2. Fold the paper in half and then back on itself again so that the paper makes a zigzag shape.

3. Draw a Christmas tree on the first side of the paper, making sure that one set of branches touches both sides of the paper. This will be the link between the sheets.

4. Then cut out the Christmas tree shape, making sure not to cut along the folds of the paper.

5. Open up the shape, and you should have a dancing string of trees, which you can decorate with different colors and stickers. Write your message inside.

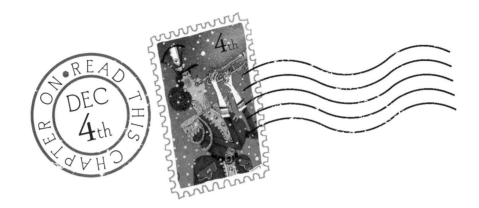

WINSTON SETS OFF

Goodness! There wasn't a moment to lose! If he was going to get this letter to the North Pole, he'd have to get going straight away!

Winston had never experienced Christmas before, but he knew all about Santa Claus. Over the past few weeks the entire world had gone Christmas-crazy. The shops were packed to the rafters from morning to night with busy-looking people bustling about with long lists and their arms full of boxes and gifts. Winston had watched, bemused. What was it all about? Who was this jolly man with the beard and the red suit whose picture seemed to be appearing everywhere?

Then one night about a week ago, Winston had found a wonderful place to sleep. It was a small den near the basement kitchen window of one of the grander houses in the city. Spots like this were always good places to spend a night, but unfortunately you couldn't stop there for long—cooks didn't like mice hanging around their kitchens. Luckily, no one had noticed Winston so he enjoyed the lovely food smells that had floated out of the open window and the great wafts of heat that rolled out every time the oven doors had been opened.

Later in the evening, when Winston had been thinking about going to sleep, the cook and the butler had rolled up their sleeves to get started washing the dishes and had popped the radio on to keep them company. Winston had been enthralled. There'd been lovely Christmas music, choirs singing, and a lot of talk about Santa Claus. Apparently on Christmas Eve this Santa Claus person put on his nice warm coat and hat and set off on a sleigh pulled by flying reindeer from the North Pole. He delivered presents to every child across the world. And all before morning!

How exciting! Winston thought. And how nice it would be to have a little fireplace all of his own to hang up a stocking. Now standing in the alleyway, Winston sighed at the thought. Then he thought of the poor child whose letter hadn't made it to Santa Claus's house. They would wake up in the morning to find no presents in their stocking or hidden under the Christmas tree.

Winston wrapped his scarf neatly around his neck again and tried to ignore the grumbling, rumbling noises coming from his tummy. This was an extremely important job.

He picked up the envelope and marched very decisively to the end of the alleyway and out into the street.

Then he stopped.

Where exactly IS the North Pole? he wondered. He knew it was north but *how* far north was it? His legs were only very small and the snow made it rather difficult to travel very quickly—especially carrying a letter with him all the way. He'd probably only have a few hours to get there, so he'd have to make sure he was going in the right direction.

All around him, people were still rushing and there were legs striding about in all directions. Tired legs belonging to commuters heading home after work; excited legs of people going out to Christmas Eve parties; and giddy little legs, mainly belonging to the smaller human beings who were running about hooting and hollering and messing about in the snow.

All of this was quite confusing for Winston who felt very tiny indeed.

"What I need," Winston squeaked to himself, "is a map."

But where could a mouse find one of those on Christmas Eve? The bookshops were closed and even the museum, which Winston knew had a great collection of very old maps, was closed until after the holidays.

Just then an idea landed rather neatly in Winston's mind. There was a shop not far away from where he was—on Mistletoe Street, he thought—that might be able to help him.

Tucking the envelope under his arm, Winston set off.

MAKE A SNOWFLAKE DECORATION

Paper snowflakes are a really nice way to decorate your house for Christmas. You can make as many as you want with lots of different types of patterns— try creating your own blizzard!

YOU WILL NEED:

WHITE PAPER

SCISSORS

1. Take a sheet of white paper, place a plate on it, and trace around it with a pencil. Cut the circle out.

2. Fold the circle in half.

3. Then fold it in half again so it makes a triangle.

4. And then fold it in half again so that it makes an even smaller triangle.

5. Once you've folded the paper three times, you can start cutting out the patterns for your snowflake! Just cut out one or two small shapes along each side of the triangle. Make sure that you don't cut out too much, otherwise the snowflake may fall apart.

6. Finally, open up your triangle to reveal your beautiful snowflake! You can stick it to a window or on presents to decorate them or maybe hang it up on the Christmas tree.

7. Try making some more and cutting out different patterns—just like real snowflakes, each of your snowflakes will be unique!

WINDOW SHOPPING

The shops on Mistletoe Street had closed their doors for the evening but there was still plenty going on. People were strolling around and the band on the corner was playing jolly Christmas music with such enthusiasm that it made Winston's tiny toes tap and his heart bounce to the beat as he crunched through the snow with the letter.

The street was looking particularly beautiful tonight.

It was one of the oldest streets in the city—a hodgepodge of buildings all cobbled together so tightly and in such a ramshackle way that you felt that with just one strong gust of wind they could all topple over like dominoes.

Tonight it looked more magical than ever, as if a giant baker had made the buildings out of huge slabs of gingerbread and sprinkled them with sugar. With the snowflakes falling and the ropes of twinkling lights strung among the bare winter trees, it was like a Christmas card.

Winston knew he had to be quick but he couldn't help looking into the shop windows as he walked by.

First, unfortunately for Winston's rumbling stomach, was the bakery. It was a three-story building that grew narrower with each floor so that it looked a like a three-tiered wedding cake. Winston looked dreamily at all the cakes and treats displayed in the enormous window at the front of the store. There were large Christmas cakes covered with gleaming white icing as smooth as a frozen pond. Some were decorated with Christmas-tree cookies, and one cake had a large edible snowman sitting on top of it!

Dancing around the cakes were gingerbread men and women. Winston knew they were only made from dough but he wished he could slip through the window and dance with them. The centerpiece of the display was an enormous gingerbread castle, golden brown and dusted with sugar. Shiny sweets had been melted down to make the windows so that a light shining from inside made them look like real stained glass glinting in the moonlight. Winston's tummy growled loudly at the smells—marzipan, ginger, plump soaked cherries, and perfectly baked cakes—which wafted temptingly from the gap under the door. (It was just too narrow for him to squeeze under...)

Reluctantly, he turned and kept going down the street.

He passed the tailor's with the dressmaker's mannequins standing in the window modeling outfits perfect for the cold winter weather.

There were bolts of fabric propped up behind them and a collection of pretty sewing baskets overflowing with shiny buttons and trimmings.

Winston had become quite attached to the scarf he was wearing but he decided that a little coat made out of the cozy blue velvet on display would really look quite nice on him and keep him snug too!

He scampered on. Next came the candy shop with its enormous glass jars filled with all sorts of delicious-looking treats and, in the middle of the display, a fat little fir tree covered with candy canes. Winston thought it looked so pretty with its confectionery decorations, even if he wasn't completely sure why there was a tree INSIDE the shop.

An icy blast of air suddenly shivered down Mistletoe Street. It took Winston by surprise and made his ears blow inside out. As he struggled to fix them, the envelope in his paws escaped and danced off down the street.

He squeaked and raced after it. With a well-judged leap he dived on it and, after a few roly-poly tumbles, he and the letter skidded to a stop outside another brightly lit shop. Winston dusted himself off and glanced up at the window. He stopped dead in his tracks and gasped.

He couldn't believe what he was looking at.

MAKE WINSTON ORNAMENTS

Winston not only makes a festive finger puppet, but he is also the perfect Christmas tree ornament! These paper ornaments are fun to make and to decorate your tree with.

YOU WILL NEED:

A SHEET OF WHITE CONSTRUCTION PAPER

YARN OR RIBBON

A HOLE PUNCH

PENCIL

A BLACK MARKER

SCISSORS

1. Look at the illustrations on page 36 to sketch a mouse shape on the sheet of construction paper with your pencil. You can make the mouse as big as you'd like. If you'd like to make a few Winston ornaments, make them small enough to fit a few on the sheet.

2. With the help of an adult, cut out the mouse shape.

3. Once the ornament is cut out, have an adult help you punch a hole near the top of the mouse's body.

4. Use the black maker to draw eyes, a mouth, and whiskers on the mouse.

5. Cut a 4-inch piece of yarn and put it through the hole in the ornament. Tie the yarn so it creates a loop.

6. Now, hang your Winston ornament on your Christmas tree!

THE ROOM
IN THE RAFTERS

It was BEAUTIFUL.

Winston was outside a toy shop and the golden glow from inside illuminated the snowy pavement around him. The window had been carefully designed so that it looked like a miniature version of Mistletoe Street. Little toy-sized shops were set up and covered in pretend snow. Beautiful dolls and teddy bears were busily going about their Christmas business. Miniature trees were covered in twinkly lights, and a little band of wind-up figures were playing a song on their tiny tin instruments. Behind the street, a toy train chugged and puffed real smoke as it made its way back and forth across the window, and a beautifully carved fairground wheel, complete with plush animal passengers, turned in time to the band's music.

All of this was wonderful, but what Winston couldn't pull his eyes away from was the towering doll's house in the middle of the scene. The front had been opened up so that you could peek at its five floors. Each room had been carefully decorated. Winston stood with his nose pressed against the glass.

Through the front door there was a hallway with a beautifully tiled floor and lamps that flickered warmly. A collection of tiny coats was hanging on a coat stand, and some rainboots no bigger than thimbles were drying on some miniature sheets of newspaper.

On the floor below, a busy kitchen scene was being played out. Little saucepans bubbled and quivered on the stoves, and every so often puffs of steam escaped from the glowing ovens. Course after course of beautiful food was cooking away ready for the party that was taking place upstairs in the dining room. This was a grand room with ornate wallpaper and a large (for a doll's house) chandelier sparkling above the long table.

Winston's eyes wandered to the comfortable library where— Winston gasped—every wall was lined with tiny books. A plump armchair with a comfy cushion and a footstool was set in front of a roaring fire. Winston could just imagine sitting in that room after dinner with a blanket over his knees, having a nice little nap with a full belly.

Upstairs was a grand bedroom, a bathroom with a deep bathtub (with real bubbles floating around), and a nursery with tiny toys and even its own doll's house!

He looked up to the final floor and sighed so deeply that a blossom of hot air momentarily fogged up the glass in front of him. He wiped it away with his paw and his eyes gleamed.

Tucked away under the sloping roof was the coziest-looking little room Winston had ever seen. It wasn't as grand or as elegant as some of the other rooms on the floors below, but to Winston it looked like the snuggliest, most beautiful room ever. There was an overflowing bookcase full of tiny books and the cozy bed was piled high with pillows, soft blankets, and even a little patchwork quilt. A lamp was glowing softly beside the bed next to a mug of steaming cocoa. Everything was perfectly to scale and just right for a doll . . .

Or a mouse, thought Winston.

How lovely it would be to live in such a place! And how exciting it would be for any boy or girl to find a doll's house like this in the morning, all wrapped up with a big bow tied around the middle.

Winston sighed again. Just imagining that scene made him feel warm from the tips of his ears to the bottom of his paws. This doll's house would make such a special present for someone.

Present . . . Christmas . . . Christmas present . . .

Winston shook himself. What on earth was he doing standing here gawking at shop windows when he had a job to do? Time was ticking away! If he didn't hurry, the letter-writer wouldn't get any presents at all. With a final glance at the attic room, he scampered off to find out exactly where the North Pole actually was.

MAKE A PAPER CHAIN DECORATION

*Paper chains are really easy to make and they are
a great way to decorate your house for Christmas!
You can hang them from the ceiling or use
them to decorate your Christmas tree.*

YOU WILL NEED:
COLORED PAPER (OR OLD MAGAZINES)
GLUE OR TAPE
SCISSORS

1. Cut your paper into thirty strips, roughly ¾-inch wide and 8-inches long. Try to make all the strips the same size, but it doesn't matter if some of them are different! You can cut as many strips as you want and your paper chain can be as long or as short as you like.

2. Once you've cut your strips, take one strip of paper and make a circle with it so that the two ends meet. Stick the ends to each other using either glue or tape.

3. Now take your next strip—if you are using colored paper choose a different color—and put it through the middle of the circle you just made. Glue or stick the ends of your second strip together so that the first and second strips are linked. This is the beginning of your chain!

4. Take a third strip and put it through the middle of the second circle and stick the ends together as before.

5. Keep repeating this process until you have used up all your strips of paper. You can cut out more strips if you want to make your paper chain longer.

6. And that's it! Now you can ask a grown-up to hang your paper chain for you.

7. It's so easy to make paper chains. You can try decorating your paper with drawings or stickers before you cut it into strips!

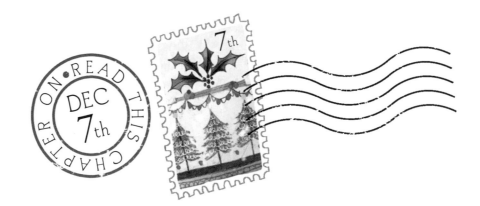

THE JOLLY HOLIDAY
TRAVEL AGENTS

T he shop Winston had actually been looking for was a little further down the road where Mistletoe Street turned and all the buildings started to wiggle down a bit of a hill. It was a small skinny shop that was wedged between a pie shop (the smell of warm pastry wafting out from under the front door was almost too much for Winston) and a wool shop (which had a funny display in the window of mechanical sheep in fuzzy sweaters leaping over knitted presents).

But what Winston was most interested in now stood before him. He read the words painted above the window carefully.

THE JOLLY HOLIDAY TRAVEL AGENTS.

. . . and underneath:

Say Bonjour! Ciao! ¡Hola! Hej Hej!
to the Whole Wide World!

Yes, this was definitely the place Winston needed if he was going to find out exactly where the North Pole was and how to get there.

Winston scampered closer and peered carefully at all the photographs that were hanging in the window. Each one was different and as Winston studied them he tried to remember everything he had heard about the North Pole on the radio. It was apparently very, very cold and snowy. Santa Claus's only neighbors would be polar bears!

Winston could feel a nervous wiggly-jiggly sort of feeling starting to flutter in his tummy. None of the pictures showed anywhere that looked right. All the photographs were of hot, sunny places. There were photos of boats sailing past sandy beaches and pictures of cities full of towering buildings that reached up into the sky. There was no snow anywhere.

What am I going to do? he thought to himself. His cheeks were glowing red as a little wave of worry started to rise from the tips of his toes all the way up to his ears.

He noticed that each of the pictures had a thin strand of gold thread attached to it which stretched across the window to a large model globe in the middle of the scene. The threads showed you where each of the exotic places shown in the pictures was located on the globe.

Winston was just thinking that none of that helped him very much when he noticed two white patches on the globe. One at the bottom and one at the top. *White,* Winston thought. Like the snow all around him.

"I wonder . . ." he squeaked to himself and a little burst of excitement went off in his chest like a firework.

He dashed over to the drainpipe and stashed the envelope carefully behind it. Then he clambered up the metal pipe and, wiggling just for a second to judge the distance right, leaped on to the window ledge. When he got to the middle he wiped away the little patch of fog caused by his breath and peered in at the globe. The spot of white at the bottom said "Antarctica," and under that, "South Pole." Winston's nose wiggled excitedly. If the South Pole was at the bottom he would bet his whiskers on the other patch of white being the North Pole! Of course he thought he'd better just check.

With a nimble leap Winston managed to jump up and grab hold of the leading between the panes of glass. He pulled himself up on to it, wobbling slightly as there wasn't really enough room for him to stand properly. With another leap and a heave he was standing on the next length of leading where he was able to look down on to the globe.

"Yippee!" squeaked Winston when his eyes had darted across the white continent and seen what was written there: the ARCTIC. . . and the North Pole! He'd found it!

But his excitement was short lived. It was an awfully long way away. A very long way away indeed. How would he, with his tiny paws, travel all that way before midnight?

His brain was racing. He was trying to think of a solution to this problem when he heard a noise coming from behind him. His body stiffened against the glass and his ears twitched nervously.

Then a loud voice said, "WHAT ON EARTH DO YOU THINK YOU ARE DOING?"

Winston was so surprised that his little feet slipped this way and that along the icy window leading. His tiny arms windmilled wildly as he tried to balance and his paws grabbed madly at the glass. But it was no use. With a loud, startled squeak Winston slipped and found himself falling backward through the chilly air until he landed ears-deep in the snow below.

INTERNATIONAL CHRISTMAS TRADITIONS

People all over the world celebrate Christmas in lots of different and wonderful ways. Many countries have their own Christmas traditions and here are just some of the amazing ways festivities take place around the world.

ICELAND

In Iceland, it is traditional for family and friends to give each other books on Christmas Eve. They will then spend the rest of the night reading their books and eating chocolate. This tradition is part of a season called *Jolabokaflod*, which can be translated as "The Christmas Book Flood."

AUSTRALIA

In Australia, the weather is usually very hot during Christmastime, so people celebrate on the beach! In the weeks leading up to Christmas, lots of festive picnics and carol services take place on many different beaches around the country.

VENEZUELA

In the city of Caracas in Venezuela, all the streets are closed on Christmas morning. This is because every year on Christmas Day hundreds of people put on their rollerskates and skate to church! Sometimes on Christmas Eve, children will tie a piece of rope to their toes and let the other end dangle out of the window. The next morning the skaters tug on their rope as they go past, waking up the children so that they can watch the amazing spectacle from their windows!

PORTUGAL

In Portugal, families traditionally gather together to eat the *Consoada* on the evening of Christmas Eve. It usually consists of fish, potatoes, eggs, and broccoli or kale.

ETHIOPIA

Ethiopians celebrate Christmas on January 7th. People wear white clothes and the men and boys play a game called *ganna*, which is played with sticks and wooden balls (similar to hockey). Traditional Ethiopian Christmas foods include *wat*, a spicy and thick stew. (Sounds yummy!)

THE PHILIPPINES

In the Philippines, there is a special Christmas tradition of having a Christmas *parol*. This is a special lantern in the shape of a star which represents the star of Bethlehem. The *parol* is made of bamboo and paper and is a very important symbol of Christmas in the Philippines—as important as the Christmas tree is in Western culture!

THE NETHERLANDS

People in the Netherlands celebrate the name day of Saint Nicholas, who is known as Sinterklass. On the night of December 5th, children will put their clogs by the fireplace. If they've been good, Sinterklass will leave some chocolate in their clogs—sometimes this can be a giant chocolate letter, usually the first letter of their name!

THINKING BIG THOUGHTS

Oh no! thought Winston, glumly from upside down and tummy-deep in a snowdrift.

Then he felt a tight pinch on the end of his tail and found himself being plucked free from the snow. A shiver of dread shimmied down his whole body and he squeezed his eyes shut tightly so he couldn't see who or what was pulling him free.

I'm probably going to be gobbled up! He panicked.

But no gobbling came.

Not even a nibble.

Instead, he was placed carefully on the ground. After a few seconds he decided to be brave and peek through his eyelashes.

"Oh!" he squeaked, opening his eyes wide.

What was standing in front of him wasn't a monster about to eat him up—but a pigeon. A big plump pigeon who was looking at him with her head tilted to one side.

"Oh good!" she cooed. "You're okay! I was so worried for a moment. I didn't mean to startle you and make you fall but we were sitting up there—" she flapped a wing in the general direction of a bare winter tree, "and I said to myself, 'Now, what's going on there, Edna?'—I'm Edna, by the way—And I saw you start to climb up those windows, and I said, 'There's going to be a terrible accident in a minute,' what with you being so tiny and climbing so high and those windows in this weather can be very slippery. So I said to myself, 'I'm going to go and see what's happening!' Didn't I, George? George!"

Edna squinted up at the tree again.

"Oh!" she eventually continued. "He's still up there." Then she squawked "GEORGE!" so loudly that Winston almost found himself knocked off his feet again.

A couple of seconds later a sleepy and slightly grumpy voice came from the tree, accompanied by some fluttering. "All right! I'm on my way! Keep your feathers on!"

A short moment later a robin landed next to Winston. Well, he thought it was a robin because it had pretty red feathers on its chest. But it was so plump it looked like a small feathery tennis ball with a beak and two tiny stick legs coming out of the bottom of it.

"This is George," said Edna.

"I'm George," George yawned.

"As I was saying," continued Edna, "we saw you and wondered what on earth you were up to! It's Christmas Eve—you should be tucked in asleep somewhere cozy."

"Well, yes . . ." said Winston. "But, you see, I have a Very Important Job to do tonight!"

He dashed over to fetch the envelope and showed it to Edna and George.

He explained all about how he'd found it and that he needed to deliver it to Santa Claus at the North Pole before midnight.

"That's when he takes off to deliver all the Christmas presents across the world," Winston said. He glanced back up at the travel agent's window and sighed. "But the North Pole is an awfully long way from here. According to that globe up there it's across an ocean and I don't think I'll be able to find a boat to get me there in time. It's already getting quite late . . ."

Saying that out loud suddenly made Winston feel very sad and disappointed. If the envelope didn't get there in time, whoever had written the letter wouldn't have a very merry Christmas the next day.

Edna saw Winston's whiskers wobble and his ears go a bit floppy. He looked so forlorn and droopy. *Well,* she thought. *That just won't do.*

"Now," she said, "let's not get ourselves down in the dumps! Every problem has a solution, doesn't it George?"

George, who had been snoozing against Edna, woke then quickly agreed with her. "Oh yes!" he said. "A solution!"

Edna wandered around in a circle thinking Big Thoughts, then let out an excited squawk! "Oh! How silly I've been!" she cried, fluffing herself up. "Follow me!" And with that, she started to stalk very briskly down Mistletoe Street.

Winston looked at George and George looked at Winston.

They didn't know what was happening but they realized that the best thing would be to do as she said. Winston tucked the envelope under his arm again then he and George started off down the street after their friend.

"Are we going to the North Pole?" Winston panted as he scampered behind Edna.

"No!" cooed Edna, without slowing down. "No need to go there my dear—I'm pretty sure that Santa Claus is already here in the city!"

To Santa Claus
Candy Cane Lane
The North Pole HOHOHO

MAKE A POM-POM ROBIN

Make yourself a fluffy pet robin out of pom-poms!
You could use this robin as a Christmas decoration.

YOU WILL NEED:
CARDBOARD TO MAKE TWO RINGS
(A CEREAL BOX IS PERFECT FOR THIS)
A PENCIL
BROWN YARN
SCISSORS
GLUE
WHITE, YELLOW, AND RED PAPER TO MAKE EYES,
A BEAK, AND TUMMY

1. First, you'll need to draw two identical circles on your cardboard. Place a coffee mug on the cardboard and trace around the rim of the mug. Repeat. Cut both circles out carefully.

2. Place a small measuring cup in the middle of each circle and trace around its rim. Ask a grown-up for help with the next part. They will need to make a cut from the outside of the circle to the center and then cut out the smaller circle. The pieces of cardboard will be in a ring shape. (They should look like donuts.) Stack the two rings on top of one another.

3. Take a very long piece of brown yarn—roughly twice as tall as you are.

4. Poke one end of the piece of yarn through the middle of the circles and wrap it around the whole ring as many times as you can. Keep looping around the yarn you have already wrapped as this will make your robin nice and fluffy!

5. Ask a grown-up for help with the next part. They will need to cut the whole way around the yarn at the outer edge of the ring until you can carefully pull the two cardboard rings slightly apart. This can be tricky so it's best to use small, sharp scissors.

6. Take a length of yarn and tie it in a knot between the two cardboard rings. Tie it tightly to secure your pom-pom as this will hold all the threads of yarn in place.

7. Now pull off the rings of cardboard and fluff out your pom-pom to reveal the body of your robin—your yarn will spring back to make a ball!

8. Finally, cut a diamond shape out of the yellow paper, folding it in the middle to create a beak. Cut two circles out of the white paper for the eyes and a circle out of the red paper for the tummy. Stick them onto the pom-pom using your glue. Now you have a fluffy little robin! (What are you going to name it?)

COOKIES AND MOVIES

Winston didn't have a chance to ask any more questions as it was all he and George could do to try and keep up with Edna. She was waddling and fluttering as fast as she could down Mistletoe Street and around the corner on to the large busy road that cut a long wiggly line through the city.

"I'm confused!" Winston panted. "How can Santa Claus be here? He should be in the North Pole getting himself ready to take off."

"Aha!" cried Edna. "*Should* be. But what if he isn't? When you said about him being in the North Pole this evening, I thought, 'That's strange,' but didn't know why . . . Then I remembered! He couldn't be in the North Pole because I'd seen him earlier. We both had, hadn't we, George?"

George didn't reply because he was too busy huffing and puffing and wafting his hot face with one of his wings.

It didn't stop Edna though. She carried on talking.

"Me and George don't fly around as much as we used to, do we dear? Not at our age. But one thing we do like to do is go to the Empire, don't we George?"

George had just about got his breath back enough to say, "Yes, the Empire."

"What's that?" asked Winston, feeling bamboozled.

"It's a movie theater. You know: movies! The flicks! When the ticket man isn't looking we sneak in! It's nice and warm in there and so dark that nobody notices you. There's a bakery next door and we have a good feast on all the broken cookies and cake crumbs out back, then in we go to the movie theater. I like watching movies and George likes having a nice nap in the warm theater, don't you dear?"

George was asleep again.

Winston had no idea what any of this had to do with Santa Claus and the North Pole but he carried on listening as best he could. Edna had paused to catch her breath and to get her bearings.

"Yes—this way!" she cried and started waddling and fluttering down the road again.

Winston hurried after her, followed by George who may or may not have been actually sleepwalking.

"We went there this morning and that's where I saw him—Santa Claus!" Edna continued.

"At the movies?" asked Winston, his eyes like saucers.

"No," said Edna. "Outside. And with any luck he'll still be there!"

As she said that she rounded a corner with Winston and George still tagging along behind her. They were now at a very busy intersection where several roads all came together. All around them were movie theaters and restaurants and shops. Lots of people were strolling around and bright lights glittered everywhere. Winston spotted the Empire movie theater with its name written in huge letters filled with electric light bulbs.

"Aha!" hooted Edna all of a sudden, sounding very pleased with herself. "There he is!"

Winston squinted. He could see lots of people but none of them were dressed in red with a big fluffy white beard. "Where?"

Edna grinned.

"Look up!" she cooed.

MAKE CHRISTMAS GIFTS

LAVENDER BAG

A homemade lavender bag is a great present for friends and family and it will keep its lovely smell for ages! Or if you'd rather keep it for yourself you can put it in a drawer or closet to keep your clothes smelling nice.

YOU WILL NEED:
DRIED LAVENDER

A PIECE OF FABRIC

RIBBON

BLACK PEN

1. Find a medium-sized bowl and place it on your piece of fabric. Trace around the rim with the black pen.

2. Very carefully cut out the circle of fabric. (Ask a grown-up for help with this.)

3. Now place your circle of fabric on a table and carefully put one spoonful of dried lavender in the middle.

4. Gather up the edges and hold them together at the top. Ask someone to hold the edges together while you tie the ribbon around the neck. Make sure you tie it as tightly as you can!

5. And there you go. You have now created your very own lavender bag. They look lovely and smell really great.

GIFT CALENDAR

A homemade calendar is a perfect personal gift for any family member.
They will be able to use it all year long by just tearing off a page
on the calendar each month.

YOU WILL NEED:
A PLAIN TEAR-OFF MONTHLY CALENDAR
(YOU CAN BUY THESE ONLINE)
A PIECE OF WHITE PAPER
GLUE
PENCILS OR PENS FOR DECORATING
(A PHOTO IS GOOD TO USE AS WELL)

1. Start by making the background for your calendar. Lay your piece of paper landscape on the table. Now you can pretty much decorate the paper in any way you would like! If you have a nice photo you can stick that in the middle. Or you could write a poem or stick your hand in some paint and print your handprints on the paper.

2. Once you've designed the center of your card you can decorate the outer edges. Try drawing something Christmassy to jazz it all up!

3. Finally, use some glue to stick the back of the calendar to the bottom of the paper.

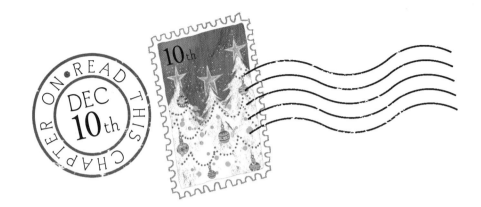

AN IMPORTANT CLUE

Winston craned his neck to see what Edna was pointing at. Attached to the side of one of the large buildings overlooking the busy traffic roundabout were lots of enormous signs advertising various things: theaters, cafés, chocolate bars, and even expensive, snazzy socks. Some of the signs were completely lit up; others had light bulbs all around them flashing on and off at different intervals; some had words in fancy light-up writing that flickered brightly against the dark night sky.

In the middle of all of this was what Edna had wanted to show Winston. On a huge advertising board, which must have been at least twenty feet high, was the smiling jolly face of Santa Claus! It was definitely him! He had the white fluffy beard, happy twinkly eyes, and

the red velvet suit that looked very warm and cozy.

Winston's heart lifted. Then it plummeted again. This wasn't the real Santa Claus. It was just a nice picture of him in an advertisement. Winston said this sadly to Edna.

Edna chuckled. "Oh you are a silly mouse!" she said kindly. "Of course it's just a picture. But I think it might also be a clue as to where you can actually find him here in the city. Read the sign!"

Winston looked up again and squinted his eyes against the snow that was still falling all around him. The sign said:

FORTESQUE'S DEPARTMENT STORE
Visit Santa Claus in store today!

Winston's cheeks went pink with excitement. Could it be true? Could Santa Claus really be here in the city? He had to find out! He didn't really know what a department store was but it sounded exciting. Perhaps it was somewhere Santa Claus went to get the supplies he'd need for his long journey around the world? He'd surely need at least a couple of boxes of cookies to keep him going for the night . . .

"Do you know where Fortesque's Department Store is, Edna?" Winston asked, quivering with excitement.

Edna walked around in a little circle while she thought.

"I don't think it's very far from here. You'll need to cross this road VERY CAREFULLY and then just take that big road there and keep going straight down until you get to the shop. If I remember correctly, it's a big store with its name in large letters above the door."

"Will you both come with me?" asked Winston. He'd gotten quite used to having a nice friend or two with him now. It made him stop thinking about how cold his paws were and how grumbly his stomach was.

"Oh I wish I could, my dear," said Edna. "I love an adventure, but I've got to get poor George back to our nest. Look at him!"

Winston looked around and laughed. George was flat on his back with his two stick-like legs poking up in the air, and he was snoring so loudly it sounded like an engine.

"This is what a bellyful of cookies does to you!" Edna chuckled as she pecked gently at George's tail feathers to wake him up.

"Now you just continue on your adventure," she said, turning to Winston. "You seem like a brave mouse and I know you can get that letter to Santa Claus before midnight! Be very careful—and good luck!" Winston said thank you and let Edna fuss about wrapping his little scarf warmly around his neck with her beak.

Then with a little wave over his shoulder to the two birds, he picked up the envelope and set off toward Fortesque's Department Store to meet Santa Claus himself!

MAKE GINGERBREAD MEN

Enjoy these festive gingerbread men while you read a chapter from this book or watch your favorite Christmas movie!

INGREDIENTS:

½ CUP BUTTER AT ROOM TEMPERATURE SO IT IS SOFT

¾ CUP PACKED BROWN SUGAR

1/3 CUP MOLASSES

1 LARGE EGG

2 TABLESPOONS OF WATER

2 2/3 CUPS ALL-PURPOSE FLOUR

1 TEASPOON BAKING SODA

½ TEASPOON SALT

2 TEASPOONS GROUND GINGER

1/2 TEASPOON GROUND CINNAMON
½ TEASPOON GROUND NUTMEG
½ TEASPOON GROUND ALLSPICE
GINGERBREAD MAN COOKIE CUTTER
FROSTING OF YOUR CHOICE
HAND MIXER
WAX PAPER OR A COOLING RACK
DECORATIONS FOR THE GINGERBREAD MEN (SUCH AS
GUM DROPS, CHOCOLATE CHIPS, MINI CANDY CANES,
SPRINKLES)

1. Preheat oven to 350° Fahrenheit. Using a hand mixer, mix the butter and brown sugar until it is light and fluffy. Add in molasses, egg, and water.

2. In a separate bowl, mix together the rest of the ingredients (except the frosting). Then mix in the wet ingredients until a dough forms. Divide the dough in half so you have two flattened disks of dough. Refrigerate the dough for 30 minutes.

3. On a lightly floured surface, roll out each portion of dough so it is about 1/8-inch thick. Use a gingerbread man cookie cutter to cut out the cookies. Place the cookies on an ungreased cookie sheet, leaving approximately 2 inches between each cookie.

4. Bake the cookies for 8-10 minutes, until the edges are firm. Remove the cookies from the sheet and place on wax paper or a cooling rack.

5. Once the cookies are completely cooled, frost and decorate the gingerbread men, then enjoy!

A COZY BED
MADE OF STRAW

Winston was on his way. He was feeling a jumble of excitement and nerves. He was excited because it seemed as if his task of delivering his letter to Santa Claus would be accomplished much quicker and with less traveling over an ocean than he thought. But he was also nervous because he was now in the busiest part of the city.

All around him was noise and movement and flashing lights. Buses rattled down the center of the wide road and there were many lanes of honking, hooting, and sputtering automobiles whizzing past. Far below his paws, Winston could feel the underground trains rumbling and grumbling.

He weaved his way through the crowds of people on the pavement. Many of them looked like they were on their way to parties. Women in long gowns that sparkled in the headlights of the passing vehicles picked their way along the pavement on fancy high-heeled shoes. (Winston had to be very careful of those!) There were men in shiny two-tone shoes and when Winston looked up at them he saw they were all wearing suits with snazzy bow ties.

As Winston made his way through these glamorous crowds he stopped feeling nervous and started to feel very Christmassy.

"I'll deliver this letter to Santa Claus," he squeaked to himself. "Then I'll find somewhere snuggly to spend the night and have a good sleep—I'll need it after all this adventuring!"

Suddenly he heard something unusual. It was music, but not like the loud jazzy music that had been floating out of the restaurants he'd just scurried past. This was gentle, like a lullaby. Winston stopped to listen for a moment, his ears waggling like antennae trying to find out where it was coming from. He followed the sound and found it was coming from an old building with a tall pointy tower that was set slightly back from the main road. A soft, warm, flickering light was coming from within and Winston sneaked in through a gap in the door.

The inside of the building was beautiful and Winston was transfixed by the carved ceiling and colorful stained-glass windows. Hundreds of candles flickered softly making the whole place feel very peaceful. He wasn't alone. The building was full of people sitting on long benches listening quietly to a choir at the front singing beautiful music. Winston knew some of the words because he'd heard them being played on the radio and by bands in the city. *Christmas carols*, he thought.

As he looked around, he spotted a curious object set up nearby. It was a large toy building a bit like a doll's house but it looked more like a barn or a stable. Inside, several statues were standing on a bed of clean, sweet-smelling straw. There was a woman in blue and several men. Some were dressed in fancy clothes and others were dressed like farmers, and there were even some pretend sheep standing beside them. Everyone was looking at a tiny wooden box in the middle. It was filled with straw and inside, fast asleep, was a tiny model baby.

That does look like a nice place to sleep, Winston thought, and he yawned. Perhaps it wouldn't hurt if he just had the tiniest of naps there beside the baby? But as he began clambering into the stable scene the choir finished singing and the congregation clapped. The sudden noise made Winston stop sharply in his tracks. He wiggled his whiskers.

"Winston!" he said sternly to himself. "You can't think about taking a nap when you haven't finished your Important Job!" And with a flick of his tail, he forced himself to pad down the aisle and back out into the cold night. He thought about the little baby asleep in the wooden box full of straw and promised himself that, as it was Christmas Eve, he would come back when the letter was delivered and take a nap in that nice peaceful building while candles flickered warmly around him.

MAKE STAINED-GLASS
WINDOW COOKIES

*These cookies look and taste really special! The candies
on top makes them stand out and look really Christmassy.
This recipe makes twelve cookies.*

INGREDIENTS:
2 CUPS PLAIN FLOUR
½ CUP BUTTER
½ CUP CASTOR SUGAR
COLORED HARD CANDIES

1. Make sure you wash your hands before you start.

2. Ask a grown-up to preheat the oven to 320° Fahrenheit.

3. Line a tray with parchment paper. This is so the cookies don't stick.

4. Put the flour, butter, and sugar in a mixing bowl and then mix all the ingredients together using your hands.

5. When the mixture starts holding together, shape it into a ball. You've just made your own cookie dough. Cover the bowl and put it in the refrigerator for twenty minutes.

6. Roll the dough out with a rolling pin until it is roughly as thick as your middle finger and use festive cookie cutters to cut out any shapes you like! Once you have cut out all your shapes, put them on to the baking tray.

7. Cut a hole in the middle of each cookie with a small cutter. Ask a grown-up to help you with this!

8. Now is the really fun part! Put your hard candies into a clean dish towel—one color per towel—then crush them lightly with a rolling pin, until they are all broken up.

9. Sprinkle a teaspoon of crushed hard candies into the hole in each cookie.

10. Put them in the oven for ten to fifteen minutes.

11. Once they are cooked let them cool and then enjoy! They will look really great and taste even better!

SPLASH AND SPLATTER!

Winston continued scampering down the road to Fortesque's as fast as he could. His breath billowed out in front of him in great plumes of warm fog. He imagined for a moment that he was one of the enormous trains that huffed and puffed in and out of the city from the busy stations dotted around town. His feet pitter-pattered along the pavement and, with his important letter tucked under his arm, Winston felt a bit giddy knowing that his mission would soon be completed.

He noticed that some of the people he passed were carrying boxes wrapped in the fanciest paper, many of which were adorned with ribbons and bows. He wondered what could be inside the packages? What surprises lay inside for the recipients when they ripped off the paper in the morning?

Winston wiggled his ears with excitement. With any luck, if he did his job right, the writer of the letter he was carrying would be waking up to similarly dressed presents in the morning because he, Winston, had done a good job.

Unfortunately, Winston's excitement didn't last long. As he pattered along the pavement thinking about silk ribbons and sparkly paper, a bus full of excited Christmassy people whizzed toward him. As it drew near, the driver accidentally steered just that little bit too close to the edge of the road where slushy, half-melted muddy snow was lying in a big puddly mess.

The wheels splashed icy water up in the air, which then splatted across the pavement. Most of the people managed to hop out of the way in time, but not Winston. The slush landed all over him. It was freezing cold and not one bit of him escaped it. He was coated from nose to tail in filthy, icy water.

Winston shook himself and wiped his eyes with the back of a paw. Thankfully, because the letter he was carrying had been rolled up under his arm, it wasn't too splattered with muck. Winston unravelled it and gave it a good shake. But this was his big mistake. He heard another van whizzing along the street beside him. There was no way Winston was going to be splattered again, so he dived out of the way. But the envelope slipped out of his wet paws! It was lifted high into the air above him before being snatched by a chilly puff of wind.

"NO!" squeaked Winston. He leaped up to try to grab it, but it was too high. Horrified, all Winston could do was stand covered in dripping muddy puddle water and watch as the wind blew the letter into the road. It fluttered about, buffeted against the sides of vehicles, and whipped off windscreens by wind shield wipers before slapping to a halt against the traffic-light pole in the middle of the street.

He had to get it back and the only way to do that was to cross the busy road and try to not get himself squished in the process!

Winston gulped.

MAKE WRAPPING PAPER AND GIFT TAGS

Homemade wrapping paper is really special and is fun to make! Here are two ideas you can use for making and designing your own.

YOU WILL NEED:

LARGE SHEETS OF COLORED PAPER

WHITE AND GREEN PAINT

MARKERS

A POTATO

CHRISTMAS-TREE COOKIE CUTTER

SNOWMAN WRAPPING PAPER

1. Lay your large sheet of paper on the table in front of you.
2. Put the white paint into a bowl—you're going to be using your finger to paint the paper so it's going to get messy!
3. Dip your finger into the bowl and paint a snowman on the paper—two circles, one on top of the other.
4. Repeat this shape all over the paper.
5. Once the paint is completely dry, use a black marker and draw a hat, arms, eyes, and a mouth onto each snowman. You can even add black spots for buttons on their tummies! If you have an orange marker you can add a carrot for their noses.

CHRISTMAS TREE WRAPPING PAPER

1. This activity is really fun and uses a potato to decorate your paper!
2. Ask a grown-up if they can cut a thick slice from the middle of a raw potato.
3. Press a Christmas-tree cookie cutter into the potato, so that the cut out is Christmas-tree shaped.
4. Lay the large sheet of paper on the table in front of you.
5. Put some green paint into a bowl and dip the potato in. Press the tree shape onto the paper and repeat until it is covered with Christmas trees.
6. When the paint is completely dry, use some markers to decorate your trees with ornaments. When you are happy with your paper you can use it to wrap up all your Christmas presents!

GIFT TAGS

Making your own tags for your presents is a really easy way to make your gift extra special. It is also a great way to use up old Christmas cards!

YOU WILL NEED:
SCISSORS
OLD CHRISTMAS CARDS
A HOLE PUNCH
RIBBON OR STRING
PENCILS OR PENS

1. Look through the old Christmas cards and choose the ones with the best pictures—or simply the cards that you like the best and that you think will make great tags!

2. Cut around the picture using the scissors—be very careful here and ask a grown-up for help if necessary.

3. You can cut the tags into whatever shape you would like: rectangle, square, circle, triangle, or star. If there is any writing on the back of the picture, simply glue it onto a piece of white paper and then cut around it again, so that the paper acts as a backing for your tag.

4. Make a small hole using the hole punch. Make sure the hole is near the edge of the tag so that you have plenty of room to write your message.

5. You can decorate your tag with any stickers you have or you can draw Christmassy pictures on it. Make sure you write who the present is for and wish them a Merry Christmas! Sign your name at the bottom.

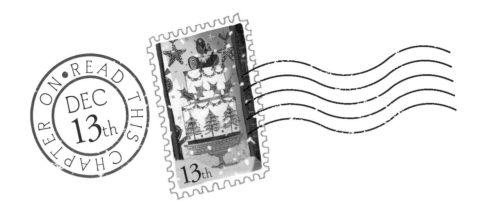

AS FLAT AS A
PANCAKE (ALMOST)

"Come on, Winston," he squeaked to himself. "You can do this!" But Winston didn't feel as if he could. The road was wide and very busy with traffic whizzing up and down it and the ground was slushy and slippery.

In the distance, the letter was still stuck to the pole. The edges were twitching and wiggling as cars zoomed by, but so far, it hadn't flown off any further down the street into the oncoming vehicles.

Winston willed his whiskers to stop shivering.

He took a few steps forward so that his feet were right on the edge of the curb. It WAS very dangerous for a tiny mouse like him to scamper into the road. He was too small for any of the drivers to see him and even more invisible against the swirling snow and bright, flashing headlights. As he watched, the lights blurred together and shimmered like the chains of fairy lights that were wrapped and looped around the street lamps and trees on either side of the road. Normally he would have thought that it all looked rather pretty, but the only thought filling his mind at this moment was how big, wide, and scary the space was between him and the letter.

He squeezed his eyes shut for a moment. "You can do it!" he told himself again. "You are a very brave mouse!"

And, he thought, maybe this was true. Usually at this time of night he would be tucked up in a hidey-hole somewhere trying to sleep and stay warm, but tonight he'd already been doing lots of brave things. Winston braced himself. He was going to do it. He was going to retrieve the letter. Looking in the direction of the traffic, he spotted a small break in the line of vehicles and chose just that moment to leap off the curb and dash part of the way across the road.

His heart was really pounding now.

He was stuck in the middle of two lanes of traffic. Cars whipped past him on both sides. The earth shuddered under his paws and great clouds of dirty black smoke coughed out from the exhaust pipes. Winston tried to focus on getting across the next bit of road and onto the small strip of raised pavement in the middle. He steeled himself, wiggled his nose, and checked for a safe gap. He took a deep breath and scampered as quickly as he could across the slippery street. But he had misjudged the speed of the cars zooming down the road. It was disorienting. A bus whizzed by and Winston spun around several times on the spot . . .

When he eventually managed to steady himself, he didn't know where he'd come from or where he was meant to be going. He heard a loud roar behind him. He squeaked in alarm—an enormous car was heading straight for him! Its bright yellow headlights were blinding and they were getting nearer and nearer. If he didn't move he'd end up as flat as a pancake.

"WINSTON! MOVE!" he cried out to himself. But his tiny feet were frozen with fear. He crouched lower on the ground and put his paws over his head. He braced himself for a collision with the car and closed his eyes tight.

He could feel the car coming closer.

And closer.

And closer.

MAKE CHRISTMAS CLOTHESPIN DOLLS

These little dolls are perfect for perching on the Christmas tree or on top of presents, and are great to give as gifts.

YOU WILL NEED:

A WOODEN CLOTHESPIN

MARKERS

FABRIC CIRCLE (ABOUT 6 INCHES IN DIAMETER)

RUBBERBAND

THIN, SPARKLY PIPE CLEANER

(OR GLITTER TO DECORATE A NONSPARKLY ONE)

ALUMINUM FOIL

DOUBLE-SIDED TAPE

SILVER CARDBOARD (OR ORDINARY CARDBOARD COVERED IN ALUMINUM FOIL)

1.   Draw your doll's face and hair on the clothespin.

2.   Make a small hole in the fabric—just big enough to squeeze over the doll's head. Pull it down and secure with an a rubberband. (If you don't have fabric you could use a paper napkin, a thick tissue, or a paper doily.)

3.   Make a sash from a folded piece of aluminum foil. Cover the rubberband with this and secure at the back with double-sided tape.

4.   Cut a pair of wings out of the silver cardboard (or plain cardboard covered in aluminum foil) and secure to the back of your doll with double-sided tape.

5.   Twist the pipe cleaner around the neck twice for arms. Then attach the doll to the Christmas tree.

You could also try making a Christmas angel. Use white or silver fabric for the skirt and aluminum foil for the sash. Give your doll hair made from yarn and make a halo out of an extra sparkly pipe cleaner that you twist into a halo shape and attach to the back of the doll.

Or perhaps you could make a Santa Claus doll. Use red crêpe paper for his clothes and hat, yarn for his beard and the trimming on his outfit, and black felt for his boots. Don't forget to make him a felt sack too, stuffed with newspaper or tissue to look like presents!

YOU AREN'T A SALMON

All of a sudden, Winston felt himself being picked up gently by his tatty scarf and flung across the street on to the snowy pavement.

He landed heavily and rolled across the frozen ground. He just lay on the floor panting and willing his heart to stop thumping like a big bass drum. Without opening his eyes, he patted himself down with his paws. He didn't feel as flat as a pancake, so what had happened?

He took a deep breath, opened his eyes, and nearly fainted. Standing over him, with her face very close to his own, was a large, fluffy white cat! He panicked, squeaked in alarm, and scrabbled backward as quickly as he could, keeping his eyes on the feline fiend who was glaring at him.

But instead of pouncing on him, the cat suddenly plonked herself down and lazily licked a paw.

"Darling, do come away from the edge of that road," she drawled. "I'm not going to rescue you again."

Winston stopped scrabbling and scampered away from the curb, making sure to keep the cat at an escapable distance from him at all times.

"You r-rescued me?" stammered Winston.

The cat stopped grooming herself and looked at Winston.

"Of course!" she purred. "You were about to be squished flat under the wheels of one of those cars. Very careless of you, I must say!"

When Winston didn't say anything, she continued: "I live in one of the apartments near here. My people are throwing a party this evening. Lots of nice party food and lovely music, but it got rather stuffy in there, so I came out for some air. That's when I saw you from the other side of the road and could just *tell* you were about to get hit by one of these dreadful vehicles. Someone needed to help you because you weren't helping yourself."

"And now you are going to eat me?" squeaked Winston in a small and terrified voice.

The cat looked mortally offended. "EAT you?" she cried. "Now why on earth would I eat a mouse?"

"Because that's what cats do, isn't it?" said Winston quietly. "Eat mice . . ."

The cat rolled her eyes.

"Well, I don't know about that, but this cat certainly doesn't. I've never nibbled a mouse in my life! For dinner this evening I had salmon, scallops, and a little dollop of caviar. I also had some of the canapés that were being handed around at the party. It was all rather delicious! Far more tasty than a grubby mouse, I should think!"

She licked her lips at the thought of those delicious snacks she'd helped herself to from the trays laid out in the kitchen at home.

"Now tell me what you were thinking, trying to cross that busy road when you are scarcely much bigger than a walnut!"

Winston took a few steps closer to the cat who smiled at him kindly. He was feeling less afraid now. The closer he got to his rescuer, the more he could see that she wasn't pretending. Her eyes twinkled with kindness that seemed absolutely genuine. She had silky, snowy fur and a diamond collar that glinted and gleamed in the light of a nearby lamp post.

"My name's Prudence," said the cat. "Lady Prudence Merryweather-Whiskerton the Third, if you want my full title. But most people call me Pru." She eyed Winston with his grubby fur and tatty scarf. "And you are?" If she'd been wearing spectacles, she would have been looking at him over the top of them.

Winston shyly introduced himself and for the second time that evening he found himself telling his tale about the Important Mission to deliver his letter to Santa Claus, who was apparently right at this very moment in Fortesque's Department Store!

"But now I've lost the letter," he said, sighing. "So whoever wrote it isn't going to have a very merry Christmas at all, and it'll be all my fault."

Pru listened to Winston. Then she looked around, squinting as she peered across the street.

"I say," she said, "that wouldn't be it over there, would it? Stuck to that traffic light?"

Winston had to stand on tiptoes to see where Pru was pointing.

He couldn't believe it—there was the letter! Still stuck exactly where it had been all along. He'd lost sight of it when he was being spun around in circles and almost flattened. The envelope was looking a bit damp and tattered now and the writing on the front seemed a tiny bit smudged.

"Yes! That's it!" cried Winston excitedly.

Pru lowered herself down on to the snow.

"Come on!" she said, slightly bossily. "Hop on my back, and we'll go and fetch it!"

Winston wasn't sure. He hesitated, looking a bit nervous.

"For goodness sake, you aren't a salmon so I'm not going to eat you!" said Pru.

Winston laughed and carefully clambered up on to the shoulders of his strange new friend. Her fur was thick and soft and as Winston sank into it he felt warm for the first time that evening.

Once he was settled, Pru waited for a suitable gap in the traffic before bounding across the street in a few easy pounces. She leaped up and retrieved Winston's letter with her mouth and flung it over her shoulder for her passenger to catch.

"And now," she said grandly, "time for us to deliver it to Fortesque's!"

"You know where it is?" asked Winston.

Pru laughed. "Know it? Why, everything I own comes from there. It's the only place in town my people shop. They had my collar made there by the head jeweler. You'll get there much quicker if I take you. I know where I'm going—and besides, I doubt you can get anywhere quickly with such tiny feet!"

Winston laughed and held on tight as she elegantly trotted down the street. He couldn't believe that he was riding on the back of a cat.

What a strange night it had turned into!

MAKE A PARTY INVITATION

If you are throwing a Christmas party, you can make your own invitations. It's very simple and will look really nice!

YOU WILL NEED:

CARD STOCK

MARKERS

SCISSORS

1. You can make your invitations really stand out by cutting them into festive shapes! Cut the card stock into the shape of snowmen, Christmas trees, Christmas presents, or stars.

2. At the top of the invitation, write the name of the person that you are inviting.

3. Make sure that you write down where the party is taking place and what time it starts and ends. Let your guests know if you want them to dress up.

4. Sign your name at the bottom and ask them to let you know whether or not they can come.

5. Once you have written out all the information about the party on the invitations, decorate them in any way you would like. Drawings or stickers would look great.

6. When they are finished, pop them in individual envelopes and write the name of the person the invitation is for—they will love their homemade invitations!

PURVEYORS OF
FINE GOODS SINCE 1847

Traveling through the city at night on the back of a large white cat was something Winston had never ever imagined himself doing. Now that he was actually doing it, he couldn't believe how exciting and exhilarating it was!

With the rescued (and only slightly soggy) letter once again tucked under his arm, Winston gripped on tightly to his new feline friend and whizzed through the city at a terrific speed.

Now that he didn't have to make sure he wasn't about to be stepped on by a giant shoe every few seconds, Winston was able to look around and find out what the city was really like on Christmas Eve.

The first thing he noticed, or rather his tummy noticed, was the smell of glorious food everywhere. Christmas Eve parties were in full swing, and the delicious wafts of food billowing out from hotel and restaurant kitchens made Winston's belly grumble like a beast. There were roasted chestnut sellers on nearly every corner and the lovely heat from the ovens and the yummy nutty smell of the chestnuts was almost too much for Winston. He imagined leaping off Pru's back and having an impromptu winter picnic on the side of the road, gobbling up as many chestnuts as he could before he fell over with a big, full belly. Once he'd delivered his letter to Santa Claus he might be able to sneak back to one of the sellers and see if anyone had dropped any nuts on the ground.

They zipped past an enormous Christmas tree that was standing in a small square surrounded on three sides by very tall, elegant houses. The tree was decorated and bejeweled with hundreds of ornaments and glittering lights. On a rink in front of the tree, lots of people all wrapped up in scarves and hats and mittens were whizzing about on ice skates having what looked like a marvelous time. Winston wasn't sure he'd like ice skating. It was hard enough for such a tiny mouse to stand upright on snow—let alone on a sheet of ice! But it was wonderful to watch everyone having fun.

As they continued on their journey, Pru and Winston came across more shops, restaurants, and delicious smells, and Winston turned to listen to more lovely singing coming from nearby.

Pru suddenly swerved off the main road and dashed around a corner. She continued along for a short while before coming to a stop.

"There we are, young man," she said, very pleased with herself. "Fortesque's Department Store: Purveyors of Fine Goods since 1847!"

Winston looked up at the building, and his mouth dropped open. It was the fanciest, most extraordinary building Winston had ever seen. It was covered in windows—large ones on the bottom floor, with colored canopies above them, and smaller ones on the floors above. The building's grand and ornate facade seemed to shimmer and sparkle so the entire place shone brightly like a pirate's treasure chest.

"It's beautiful!" Winston gasped. "And Santa Claus is in there?"

"Well, that's what you told me!" said Pru.

"We'll head to the main doors over there and we can sneak into the shop. It'll be easy. I expect the staff will know who I am because my people are always in there and talk about me nonstop," said Pru. "Now let's get that letter of yours delivered."

Winston nodded and held on tightly to Pru's fur as she skipped nimbly across the street and headed for the beautifully polished front doors of the building.

"Here we go!" said Pru as they trotted toward the entrance. "It will be easy as p—"

But she didn't finish her sentence because right at that very moment she walked straight into the legs of a man who had appeared out of the shadows.

MAKE YOUR OWN PARTY FOOD

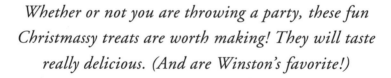

Whether or not you are throwing a party, these fun Christmassy treats are worth making! They will taste really delicious. (And are Winston's favorite!)

CHEESE STARS

INGREDIENTS:
READY-ROLLED PUFF PASTRY SHEET
1 EGG
½ CUP GRATED CHEDDAR CHEESE
FLOUR

1. Ask a grown-up to preheat the oven to 350° Fahrenheit.
2. Put a sheet of parchment paper onto a baking tray so that the stars don't stick to the tray once they are cooked.
3. Sprinkle a little bit of flour onto your work surface. Unroll the pastry sheet, and use a star-shaped cookie cutter to cut out as many stars as you can.
4. Crack the egg into a bowl and beat it with a fork until the mixture is smooth, then brush the top of the pastry stars with it.
5. Now sprinkle the cheese over the top of the stars and lift them carefully onto the baking tray.
6. Bake in the oven for ten to twelve minutes, until the stars are golden.
7. These are great to eat warm or you can store them in an airtight container for up to two days!

FESTIVE ROCKY ROAD

INGREDIENTS:
4 CUPS WHITE CHOCOLATE
¾ CUPS DRIED CRANBERRIES
½ CUP GLACÉ CHERRIES
½ CUP MINI MARSHMALLOWS
½ CUP CRUSHED GRAHAM CRACKERS

1. For this recipe you will need a dish that measures roughly 8″ x 8″.

2. Line the dish with parchment paper.

3. Melt the chocolate. Break it into small pieces and put them into a heatproof bowl. Ask a grown-up to help you place the bowl over a saucepan of gently boiling water. Turn the heat off, wait for five minutes, and then stir your melted chocolate.

4. Take the bowl off the saucepan and leave the chocolate to cool for five minutes.

5. While the chocolate is cooling you can do some smashing! Put the graham crackers in a clean dish towel and smash lightly with a rolling pin. Be careful not to hit them too hard as you don't want your graham crackers to turn into crumbs. Nice chunks of graham cracker are perfect for this recipe.

6. When the chocolate is slightly cooled, mix in your graham cracker chunks, cranberries, cherries, and mini marshmallows. Stir the mixture so that all the ingredients get nicely coated in chocolate.

7. Spoon the mixture into the dish and press it down with the back of a spoon.

8. Put the rocky road in the refrigerator for two hours and then ask a grown-up to lift the paper out and cut the rocky road into small squares. It's a really great chocolatey treat and the white chocolate gives it a great "snowy" effect that's perfect for Christmas. (It also works just as deliciously with milk or dark chocolate.)

9. The rocky road will keep in the refrigerator for up to a week.

TURKEY PINWHEEL SANDWICHES

INGREDIENTS:

1½ CUPS CREAM CHEESE
4 LARGE FLOUR TORTILLAS
CRANBERRY SAUCE
1½ CUPS TURKEY BREAST
¼ CUP SPINACH, WASHED

1. Spread out your four tortillas on a large cutting board, and then spread the cream cheese on them. Make sure you use the same amount of cream cheese on each one.

2. Take your cranberry sauce and spread a thin layer on top of the cream cheese.

3. Now that you've sorted the sauce, arrange a quarter of the turkey breast over half of each of the four tortillas. You need to make sure it's only half so that the filling doesn't fall out when you roll them!

4. Finally, put a layer of spinach on top of the turkey.

5. Now that you've layered up your tortillas you need to wrap them into pinwheels. You should ask a grown-up to help you with this because it's good to have an extra pair of hands. Starting at the end that has the turkey and the spinach, roll up the tortillas very tightly. Then individually wrap them in aluminum foil so that they hold their shape, and put them in the fridge for one hour.

6. When the hour is up, take your tortillas out of the fridge and remove the aluminum foil. Slice each tortilla into twelve pinwheels.

7. Remove the turkey for a vegetarian alternative.

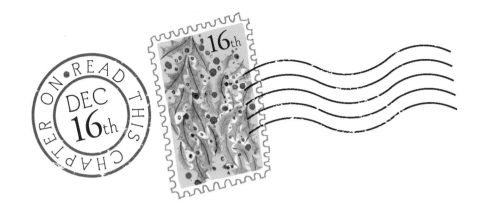

TEAMWORK

"And where do you think you're going?" said the man sternly. He glared at Pru from behind thick, round spectacles. On his jacket a badge saying "SECURITY" glinted in the moonlight.

"Hide!" hissed Pru.

Winston slid down from her back and hung upside down, clinging to the fur on her belly. Pru covered her surprise expertly and began to purr loudly, weaving in and around the man's legs and rubbing her shoulders up against the door. The security guard softened.

"What do you want to be going in to this big shop for on Christmas Eve?" he said, smiling and bending down to tickle her ears with a thickly gloved hand. "It's locked up tight for the holidays now. I just double-checked all the doors myself."

He jangled a big set of keys cheerfully.

"Now, go on—I think you should head back home. Your people will be wondering where you are! Go on. That's it—shoo!" And very gently he guided Pru away so he could finish doing his final check of the front door and head home for Christmas.

Pru purred again and made a great show of walking nonchalantly down the road with her bushy tail swishing very casually behind her.

When they were a safe distance away, Winston scrambled onto her back again.

"What are we going to do now?" he squeaked in alarm. "That man said the whole place is all locked up for the holidays."

"We'll think of something," said Pru.

Winston suddenly squeaked, "Wait! I can smell something!" He gingerly stood up on Pru's back and sniffed the night air. Yes! There was definitely something—his whiskers were wobbling, so Winston knew it must be important. What was it? He sniffed again. It smelled of nice things—flowers, soap, cookies, and candy canes and lots of other rich and delicious aromas. It all seemed to be coming from inside the department store. But where was the smell escaping from? Was there a window open? Winston let his nose twitch and sniff until it found exactly the direction they needed to go.

"Down there!" he cried. And he pointed at a very dark alley. It wasn't appealing to go down such a forbidding passage, but Pru and Winston both knew that their mystery letter-writer was depending on them.

Pru picked her way down the passage. She could smell something now too. Eventually, Winston told her to stop. He carefully slid down her silky fur and landed on the snowy ground.

"Here!" he said. "The smells are coming from here!" He pushed his way forward and revealed an air vent only a few bricks up from the floor. "I think this is a way we could get in! We can follow the smell through here until we get into the store and then we can find our way to Santa Claus. Hopefully he hasn't gone far!" Winston assessed the situation. "We need to get that grill off," he said. "I can't squeeze in through those tiny gaps."

Pru agreed. She reached a paw out and tapped the air vent experimentally. Both she and Winston jumped as it made an unexpected rattling noise.

"It's loose!" whispered Pru.

"Can you get it off?" asked Winston, watching with interest.

"I'm not sure," said Pru. "What we really need is something to undo these screws with." She stopped rattling the grill and had a good look at it up close. "I wonder . . ."

There was a flash from one of her paws as a claw suddenly appeared.

Winston gasped. It looked so sharp and shiny in the shadowy moonlight. He leaped backward away from it.

"Oh, don't be such a scaredy cat!" Pru said. "I'm going to see if I can use my claw as a screwdriver." She delicately turned the loose screw, and eventually it clattered out of its hole and fell on to the snowy ground.

"HOORAY!" Winston hooted. "Can you do the other ones? Then we can get to Santa Claus."

Pru tried her hardest on all the other screws, but they were too tight.

"It's no good," she said. "They won't budge!"

Winston sighed.

"But," said Pru, "if I pull the grill forward, you might just be able to squeeze behind it! The gap certainly looks about Winston-sized!" Winston nodded and clambered up Pru's back again. He sucked in his tummy and—PLOP!—he landed gracefully behind the grill.

"OH BRAVO, WINSTON!" purred Pru. "Here's the letter." She carefully slid the envelope through the gap to him. "Well done!" she said. "That was excellent teamwork. You'd better get a move on though—you don't want Santa Claus leaving without you!"

"Aren't you coming with me?" he said.

Pru smiled. "I'd love to, but I can't squeeze in there with you. My bottom's much too big! I'm afraid you'll have to go your own."

In the distance, church bells chimed the passing of another hour.

"Goodness!" cried Pru. "I had no idea it was so late! I'd better get back to my people! They get into a dreadful state when they can't find me."

"Thank you, Pru," said Winston. "You are the nicest cat I've ever met!"

"And you are the nicest mouse," she replied. "Now hurry along! You've got a letter to deliver!"

Winston set his whiskers at a very determined angle. Waving over his shoulder at Pru, he set off down the dark tunnel into the shop. Pru watched him until she couldn't see him any longer before trotting off into the night.

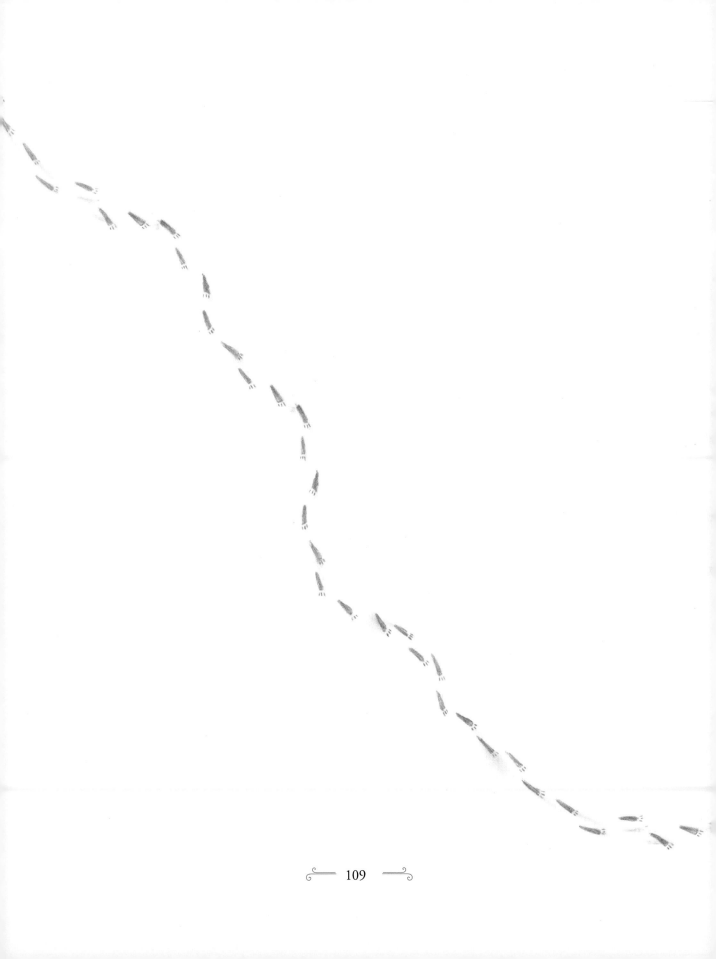

MAKE YOUR OWN CHRISTMAS TREE DECORATIONS

Making a salt dough decoration is a perfect way to get into the Christmas spirit. And even better, once you've made these decorations they will last for years!

YOU WILL NEED:

1 CUP SALT

2 CUPS FLOUR

¾ CUP WATER

1. Ask a grown-up to preheat your oven. It needs to be on the lowest possible setting, otherwise your decorations may crack!

2. Put the salt and the flour in a large bowl and mix them together using a wooden spoon.

3. Add in the water a little at a time and keep mixing. When you've added all the water, the mixture should feel like dough.

4. Put the dough onto a table and keep pressing and mixing it with your hands until it is smooth and all the ingredients have been combined.

5. Now you're ready to roll! Roll the dough out with a rolling pin until it is roughly 1/8-inch thick.

6. Use Christmas cookie cutters to make the shapes you want, then use a pencil to make a small hole at the top of each shape—this is where you will put the ribbon to hang the decoration on the Christmas tree later.

7. Now you need to bake them! Put some parchment paper on a baking sheet and then arrange your shapes on the paper.

8. Leave them in the oven for four hours so that they are fully hard.

9. When they are ready, take them out and leave them to cool.

10. Now for the fun part—decorating! Use acrylic paints (these stick well to the dough) to decorate your ornaments any way you like. When the paint is dry, put a small ribbon through the holes you made with the pencil and hang them on the Christmas tree.

DILLY-DALLYING

Winston edged his way tentatively down the tunnel. He was feeling nervous again. Pru had been an unlikely friend, but her company and help had been just what Winston had needed. Now he was all alone again and heading into the unknown world of the department store.

He thought about the security man from earlier and was worried that there might be others in the store. Would they notice him? What would happen if they caught him? And would Santa Claus still be in the store?

The smells from the store were getting stronger and stronger and it wasn't long before a dim light illuminated the way in front of him. After turning the corner, he soon came to another grill. Luckily this one was much more generous than the one in the alleyway. After rolling up the envelope and pushing it through the grill, Winston tried squeezing himself through. It wasn't easy but after a few minutes of sucking in his tummy, folding up his ears, and huffing and wiggling he popped out of the tunnel like a cork from a bottle of champagne and went tumbling, tail over ears, across the floor. He picked himself up and scurried back to collect his precious letter. It was only after he had stopped and listened for any human footsteps—and not heard any approaching—that he allowed himself to breathe properly and look around.

He was in a vast room. Thick, fluffy carpet stretched out as far as he could see. Around him on all sides were well-polished counters and, if Winston went on tiptoes and really stretched his nose high, he could just about see what was displayed on top of them in their shiny glass cases.

There were hats of all colors and designs, gloves of all lengths and fabrics, silky scarves and handbags all lined up in rows.

As Winston padded along, he gazed at it all in awe. The building itself was beautiful, with carved wooden columns holding up the high-vaulted ceiling. Although the main lights were off, hundreds of pretty Christmas garlands of holly, with ornaments, and tiny presents nestled among them, were strung along every surface, their fairy lights twinkling and sparkling, making the whole place look like a glittering, magical grotto.

The smells Winston had sniffed outside were almost overwhelming now that he was inside the building. They tumbled over and around each other in his nose, and it made him feel a bit dizzy. He had to concentrate very hard to remember that Santa Claus was somewhere in the building —Winston didn't have time to be wandering about, dilly-dallying!

Hitching the letter securely under his arm, Winston marched off determinedly. He had absolutely no idea where he was meant to be going, but he felt that if he just kept walking sooner or later he would find something that would tell him where he was and where he might find Santa Claus.

And he was (sort of) right.

After several minutes of walking between the display cabinets and mannequins, the room opened up into a huge atrium. Winston craned his neck and looked up and around him. Enormous richly carved banisters and thickly carpeted staircases wound their way up and around the space leading the customers to the treasures that were on sale on the other five floors. At the top, the building was finished off by a great glass dome from which hung a gigantic crystal chandelier.

A large Christmas tree, lit up and decorated with ribbons and jewels, stood in the middle of the room. Winston spun around taking it all in.

Five floors! he thought and he felt his ears droop. How would he be able to search for Santa Claus quickly across five floors? Just the thought of climbing the endless staircase on his tiny paws made Winston feel exhausted before he had even started!

He took a deep breath. "Come on now, Winston!" he told himself. "We're almost there!"

Forcing his ears to stop drooping, Winston decided that the best

plan would be to search each floor in turn until he found Santa Claus.

He set off again, but he hadn't got very far when a delicious smell wafted from somewhere nearby. He had smelled some food from outside in the alleyway but the scent was now so strong that it stopped him completely in his tracks. His little pink nose twitched as wafts of cookies and candy canes, pies and cheeses, fresh bread, and party food all swirled around him. His stomach growled loudly like a lion. Winston's feet suddenly turned from the direction he had been traveling in and started marching him in the opposite direction toward the food.

"But the letter!" cried Winston. It was no use protesting. His nose, tummy, and feet were now in charge, and nothing was going to stop them from finding out where it was all coming from.

He found himself running back across the gentlemen's department—past shiny leather briefcases and coats and displays of silk ties of every color fanned out behind a model peacock.

He whizzed by the cashmere scarves, beautiful sweaters, and silk pajamas. He swerved around a tower of hat boxes and through an archway before coming to a sudden halt.

Winston blinked in wonder. He couldn't believe what he was seeing in front of him!

MAKE YOUR OWN CHRISTMAS CRACKERS

Everyone loves Christmas crackers and they're essential to every Christmas dinner! You can fill your homemade crackers with anything you like—jokes, hats, small toys, or sweets.

YOU WILL NEED:

3 TOILET PAPER TUBES

WRAPPING PAPER

TAPE

CRACKER SNAPS (YOU CAN FIND THESE ONLINE, BUT DON'T WORRY IF YOU DON'T HAVE THEM)

SCISSORS

PAPER

RIBBON

1. Cut an 8″ x 11″ rectangle of wrapping paper.

2. Lay the first tube lengthways in the middle of the paper. If you have cracker snaps, put one through the tube and put some tape at both ends to attach it to the wrapping paper so that it stays in place.

3. Now put your other cardboard tubes on either side of the central tube and roll your paper around the tubes. Use tape to keep the paper in place.

4. Carefully pull out both of the end tubes and keep them to make another cracker. Now you need to add your gift, hat, or joke! Feed it through one end of the tube and then tie ribbons at both ends of the crackers, just above where the central tube ends. Be careful not to tear your paper.

5. Repeat the process to make one for everyone coming for Christmas dinner.

TIP: If you don't have any cracker snaps, you can get the same effect by shouting "BANG" as loudly as possible when you pull the crackers!

Here are some ideas for what you can put inside your crackers:

* Paper hats—you can make your own.
* A small chocolate
* A small gift—a pencil or crayons would be good. You could even try fitting in a tiny pom-pom robin or a lavender bag!
* A handwritten joke—cut out small rectangles of paper and write your favorite jokes on them.

STINKY AND
THEREFORE TASTY

FOOD! Food, everywhere!

Mountains of the stuff!

Wherever Winston looked, food danced in front of his eyes: glossy fruit and vegetables in baskets; trays of crisp pastries and pies; towering displays of ornately iced cakes and golden-brown cookies, and sacks of exotic spices. A wall of wine bottles stood behind a beautiful counter. Canisters of teas with magical names were lined up like soldiers beside mounds of rich-smelling coffee beans.

There were mountains of nuts, castles of brightly filled jam jars, and a long counter bursting with every kind of sweet imaginable. Everywhere, baskets stamped with Fortesque's famous logo stood piled up in towers and arches, some with their lids open and all manner of delicious goods bursting out from inside.

There was also, realized Winston as his nose twitched wildly, CHEESE.

Somewhere in this enormous palace of food was wheel upon wheel of cheese. And from the smell of it, it was some of the stinkiest, and therefore TASTIEST you could ever imagine.

Winston's stomach growled again. It was so loud it almost knocked him over. He realized that he was absolutely famished. He couldn't actually remember when he'd last eaten properly. Whatever it had been, it couldn't possibly have been as delicious as what was on offer in the hall full of grub.

Winston bit his lip and thought. He knew he shouldn't take anything—that would be stealing—but he was so hungry it was giving him a tummy ache. The excitement of the evening so far had caught up with him and he felt his energy draining away. If he didn't eat something soon he doubted whether he'd be able to finish his mission. So Winston made a decision: he would just go and see if he could find where the cheese was and if he could find some tiny bits—crumbs really—he would eat them. He knew it was a bit naughty, but the job he had to do was really important and he thought anyone else would do the same just so they were able to complete their mission.

So Winston put the letter under his arm and took a step into the food hall.

And it was at exactly that moment someone threw a walnut at his head and shouted, "HEY!"

MAKE AN ORANGE POMANDER

This pretty decoration smells really great and looks nice hanging on a Christmas tree, but you can also use them to make fun Christmassy centerpieces for your table. Lemons or limes work well too and give a nice citrus smell!

YOU WILL NEED:

AN ORANGE

WHOLE CLOVES

A RIBBON

1. Cut two pieces of ribbon and wrap them around the orange. Tie them at the top then make a loop with the ends.

2. Your orange should now look like it is divided into four quarters and is ready to decorate with cloves.

3. If your orange is soft you should be able to stick the cloves straight into it. If not, ask a grown-up to puncture some holes in the skin with a sharp cocktail stick, a skewer, or the end of a knitting needle.

4. You can make any pattern you like, but lines running from top to bottom work well and look nice and neat.

5. When you've finished, hang your pomander on the tree or put it on a shelf. It will make everything smell lovely and will last for years!

EDUARDO FROMAGE

The walnut whistled through the gap between Winston's ears, but the shout had almost made him leap out of his skin with fright! He looked around, panting, to see who or what was hollering at him.

It was a large rat. He was hanging out over the top of one of the wicker baskets by the entrance to the food hall, looking very cross indeed. He clambered out and made his way over to Winston, who was still trying to catch his breath.

"Goodness me!" the rat was saying. "Never have I seen anything like it in my life—approaching a food-preparation area looking like you've just rolled in a muddy ditch! Just think of the germs!" Then he shuddered from his whiskers to his tail and recoiled away from Winston as though he were made of fire.

"I'm sorry," said Winston. "Have I done something wrong? I was only going to have a tiny bit of chee —"

"Wrong?" The rat snorted. "You were about to go wandering among some of the finest foods available in the world and just look at you! You're filthy! Absolutely filthy!"

Winston looked down at himself. In the warm yellow glow of the food hall's Christmas lights, he had to admit that he did look very grubby indeed. He turned his paws over and was shocked to see that their usual pinkness had disappeared under a thick layer of dirt. His ears drooped with embarrassment and, under the layer of grime, his cheeks flushed bright pink.

"I'm so sorry," he squeaked. "I'm just really hungry, and I've had quite a busy night."

The rat sniffed rather haughtily but softened when he saw how little and floppy-eared and tired Winston looked.

"Not to worry!" he said, before drawing himself up proudly. "My name, by the way, is Eduardo Fromage. I like to think of myself as the night manager here and as such, I can't have any germs getting near the grub. It would be a terrible business. You've got to be shipshape and sparkling clean to go into the food hall. Like me! Look how shiny my fur is! And smell me! That's the most expensive cologne the store sells!"

Eduardo turned around slowly on the spot for Winston to admire his glossy fur and exquisitely curled whiskers—and to take in the rather strong smell of spicy perfume and soap.

"Now let's get you scrubbed up and fed!" Eduardo said kindly. "What's your name, by the way?"

Winston told him.

"Marvelous!" said Eduardo. "Well you just follow me, and soon you'll be sparkling!"

✱

Five minutes later, Winston found himself on a gleaming white counter in another section of the department store. Instead of food, this part of the shop had all sorts of crystal bottles full of colored liquids and little pots and boxes of powders and creams as far as the eye could see. There were lots of advertisements with pictures of glamorous men and women on them and the entire place smelled of roses and summer meadows and cleanliness. There were mirrors everywhere and Eduardo stopped every few seconds to admire himself in them. Winston was startled when he saw his own reflection—he was a frightful state! No wonder Eduardo had thrown a walnut at him!

On the way, Winston had tried to explain his Important Mission, and that—as lovely as a bath would be—he had to track down Santa Claus in the store before he set off around the world in his sleigh. The trouble was Eduardo liked to talk. He talked and talked and talked and Winston couldn't get a word in edgewise!

It turned out that Eduardo had lived in the department store all his life and no one (apart from the owner, Mr. Fortesque, of course), knew the place better. When the store was closed, Eduardo spent his evenings wandering about the place making sure that everything was spick and span. Living in Fortesque's had given him quite a taste for the finer things in life. His office—as he called it—was a basket lined inside with a silk scarf and lots of lavender-scented pillows.

Eduardo explained most of this as he was filling a small sink with water. When he was satisfied there was enough in the basin he said, "Okay, Winston! In you go!"

"In there?" asked Winston, peering over the side. His only other experience with water was puddles. He unwound his scarf from his neck and gingerly clambered down and found that the water was rather warm. He paddled around in it. It was quite fun and he giggled as the water splashed about between his toes.

Suddenly a great dollop of floral-smelling cream landed on his head. Eduardo was hard at work dragging over lots of different bottles of lotions and creams and was squirting them into the sink and onto Winston. He told Winston to give his fur a good scrub.

Winston was slightly dubious at first, but he did as he was told and before long the water in the sink was murky and brown as all the dirt from the city streets came away. After a quick rinse, Eduardo helped Winston out and handed him a towel. Winston finally emerged gleaming white, his fur almost sparkling.

"Nice and clean!" announced Eduardo. "No germs and you look much better. I think it's time we had a little something to eat."

Winston didn't say anything. He didn't have to—his tummy grumbled very loudly in excitement as he followed Eduardo back to the food hall toward all that delicious-smelling grub!

MAKE A CHRISTMAS JAR

Christmas jars are a fantastic way to give presents that your family and friends will love. First decorate the jar and then fill it with presents.

YOU WILL NEED:
CLEAN EMPTY JAM JARS WITH LIDS
RIBBON
STICKERS
STICKER LABELS
SMALL GIFTS OR SWEETS TO PUT IN THE JARS
PAPER AND PENS

DECORATE YOUR JAR

- ✶ Cover it with star stickers.
- ✶ Write on the sticker to say what the jar contains and then draw a picture of the contents—Yummy Treats, Jokes etc.
- ✶ You can even draw on the jar using glass pens if you have them.
- ✶ Cover the top with a square of fabric.
- ✶ Tie a ribbon around the jar and attach a gift tag.

FILL YOUR JARS

1. HOBBY JARS

Think about who you want to give the present to as you can theme the contents to match their hobbies.

- ✶ Gardening—a packet of seeds, a poem about gardens, some plant labels
- ✶ Sewing—some pretty buttons, ribbon, a thimble, squares of fabric
- ✶ Craft—stickers, crayons, washi tape
- ✶ Hair-styling—hairbands, ribbons, and clips

2. JOKE JARS

This is a lovely way to always have something funny and cheery on hand. Fill a jar with pieces of paper with jokes or silly stories or pictures for people to pick out when they want a laugh.

3. TREAT JARS

Fill your decorated jars with a lovely treat.

- ✶ Sweets—homemade or store bought
- ✶ Art & craft—crayons, a pencil sharpener, or a tiny notebook
- ✶ Nuts

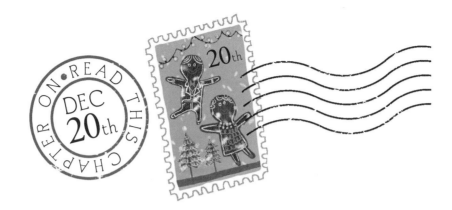

A NIGHTTIME FEAST

Back in the food hall, Eduardo and Winston decided to make a late-night picnic. They washed their paws again at one of the sinks behind the food counters before Eduardo expertly started to put together a menu. It was Winston's job to follow him around and carry the increasingly tall and wobbly tower of food they were selecting. Their feast mainly consisted of cheese—lots and lots of different kinds. There was soft cheese, hard cheese, cheese with herbs in it, and cheese with holes so big that Winston could put his head through.

"I suppose," said Eduardo, "we shouldn't only have cheese . . ." And he popped a couple of crackers on the top of the tower of cheeses then added a sliver of pie, some chunks of apple, several chocolate coins, and a large gingerbread cookie iced with a snowflake design.

"Marvelous!" cried Eduardo, thrilled with his selections. "Shall we eat?"

Winston thought he'd never ask!

The two new friends decided to set out their feast under the Christmas tree in the main hall. Eduardo had found a crisp white linen napkin and they spread it out on the floor, piling the food on top of it. Despite the vast size of the department store entrance hall, it felt so cozy to be sitting under the tree in the gentle glow of the twinkling tree lights.

Winston sat down and helped himself to a large chunk of the stinkiest cheese they had found. He was just about to put as much of it in his mouth as would fit (and maybe a bit more!) when Eduardo turned to him.

"Now, forgive me," he said, "but I don't believe you told me what you are doing in my store on Christmas Eve. Shouldn't you be tucked in asleep at home?"

Winston lowered his giant pawful of cheese and explained sadly that he didn't actually have a home.

"Ah . . . I see," said Eduardo, taking a chomp out of a buttery cracker. "Well, I'm sure it wouldn't be a problem for you to live here. There's plenty of space, and it's nice to have some company. Usually I'm just snoozing in my basket or snooping on the letters in the mail room. Very interesting!"

Letters! Post! OH NO! Winston suddenly remembered what he was meant to be doing! The letter! He'd been so busy with his bath and the picnic that he had forgotten his Important Job. He looked around—the letter to Santa Claus was nowhere to be seen. A shiver of dread ran right to the tip of his tail. He hopped up onto his feet and began pacing back and forth.

"Oh no! I've lost it! It's gone!" he squeaked.

"What's the matter?" asked Eduardo. "What's gone?"

"My letter! Well, not MY letter, but the one I was carrying. It was a big envelope and I had it with me and now I don't!"

"Oh!" cried Eduardo, catching on. "That tattered piece of paper? I tidied that away into my office before we went to get you all washed up before dinner."

Winston gasped. "I need to get it back!"

Quickly, the two new friends piled their picnic up in the napkin and Eduardo slung it over his shoulder. They raced back to Eduardo's basket. On the way, Winston twittered and squeaked his way through explaining his Very Important Mission. Eduardo couldn't believe what he was hearing!

When they got there Eduardo handed the letter back to Winston.

"Now I can deliver it to Santa Claus!" said Winston, relieved. "I hope he's still here!"

Eduardo's brow wrinkled. "Here?" he said. "In Fortesque's?"

"Yes!" said Winston. "I saw an advertisement: 'Visit him in store today!'"

Eduardo stopped, clambering back out of his basket home. He looked crestfallen.

"Oh dear, oh dear," he said sadly. "Come with me, Winston. I need to show you something very important . . ."

MAKE YOUR OWN CHRISTMAS BOX

Christmas boxes are a great way to make a gift look extra special.

YOU WILL NEED:

EMPTY CARDBOARD BOXES

WRAPPING PAPER

SCISSORS

TAPE

1. Keep an eye out for small boxes in the days leading up to Christmas. You can use a cereal box or a shoe box depending on the size of the present you want to put in it.

2. Carefully cover the box with wrapping paper and use tape to hold it in place. If the box has a lid, cover the base and lid separately.

3. You can fill your box with whatever you like—homemade treats, small toys, sweets—or use them to hold a single present.

4. Wrap your present in tissue paper and pop it in the box. Then tie the box shut with some ribbon.

5. To make it extra special, wrap the box in plain paper and cover it with your own Christmassy drawings.

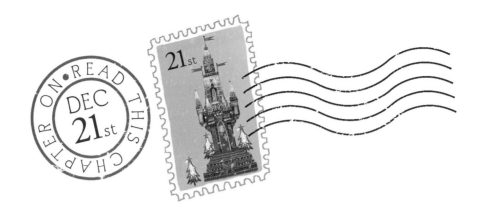

CLOCKWORK

Winston couldn't believe it.

"Mechanical?" he whispered. "It's not the real Santa Claus at all, but a mechanical one?"

He was now standing in one of the enormous windows of Fortesque's looking at the extraordinary scene in front of him. Everything was set up as if they were in Santa Claus's workshop at the North Pole. In the middle of the display stood Santa Claus but he wasn't a real person at all. He was a lovely (and probably very expensive)—model, but a model nevertheless.

"I'm afraid so," said Eduardo sadly. "We always have lovely Christmas window displays here at the store, but this is the biggest and most extravagant we've ever had. It's taken almost a whole year to plan and make. We've had crowds of people standing outside looking at it and people have traveled for miles to see it. Watch . . ." Eduardo disappeared behind one of the painted background panels and carefully flicked a number of switches that were hidden away out of sight.

The window suddenly came to life! Lights flickered on and a curtain of pretend snow began to fall behind an artificial window at the back of the workshop. Christmas music started to play and all around Winston things sprang into motion—train sets chugged around the scene puffing out smoke, toy airplanes swooped and looped overhead, rows of teddy bears waved their fluffy paws, and dolls danced in circles.

Mechanical elves dashed about on hidden tracks, each carrying presents or toys, or bunches of carrots for a reindeer whose head appeared every so often through the workshop door.

And then there was Santa Claus himself, surrounded by sacks overflowing with gifts, checking a long scrolling list in his hand, then waving to the imaginary crowds outside. His eyebrows wiggled and he smiled and every so often his big belly would jiggle with glee at the scene around him.

It really was wonderful but Winston couldn't enjoy any of it. He felt so crestfallen and sad. He'd tried so hard to deliver his letter but he'd let his hungry tummy distract him. He should have known that the REAL Santa Claus wouldn't have time to be standing around in department stores on Christmas Eve. And now it was too late to get the envelope to the North Pole.

Winston slumped against Santa Claus's boots and covered his face with his ears. "Whoever wrote that letter isn't going to get anything tomorrow morning and it's all my fault!" he groaned.

Eduardo watched Winston and felt helpless. If only there was

some way he could help his young friend out. He looked around him for any inspiration, suspecting that he wouldn't find any, but hoping nevertheless.

Suddenly, his eyes fell on something which planted the seed of an idea in his mind.

"All might not be lost, Winston!" he said slowly.

"But it is already," said Winston sadly. "I'll never get to the North Pole now."

Eduardo grinned. "I think you might!"

"How?" said Winston, sitting up.

Eduardo pointed to one of the toy planes that was busy loop-the-looping above their heads and said, "You're going to fly!"

RANDOM ACTS OF KINDNESS

Christmas is a really lovely fun time for most people, but it's important to remember people who are less fortunate and are not able to celebrate Christmas in the same way. Here are some random acts of kindness that you can try at Christmastime.

* Write a letter to someone you know who lives far away.

* Take a grown-up with you to visit an elderly neighbor and take them a yummy treat that you have cooked!

* Donate old toys that you don't play with to a charity.

* Write a card to your teacher to thank them for everything they have done for you this year.

* Do something nice and helpful for your parents or siblings.

* Add something to a food drive. Canned food is great for this.

* Stick a Christmas card on your mailbox at home with a loop of tape for your mailman. They have a very busy time at Christmas!

* Take a toy (it could be one of your stuffed toys) or some food to your local animal charity.

CHRISTMAS SCAVENGER HUNT

A scavenger hunt is a really great way to have Christmassy fun.
When you're out and about with family and friends on a walk, or
Christmas shopping—have a look and see how many things on
this list you can spot.

✶ Can you spot anyone in a snazzy Christmas sweater?

✶ Can you find a house that's covered in sparkly lights?

✶ How many Christmas trees can you see?

✶ Can you hear your favorite Christmas song?

✶ Can you see anyone drinking hot cocoa?

✶ Can you spot any dogs wearing sweaters while out for their walk?

✶ Can you see any snow? (Bonus points if it's real!)

✶ Can you see a sleigh?

✶ Can you find any Christmas cards?

✶ Can you see a reindeer? (Does it have a shiny, red nose?)

THE GREAT FLYING MOUSE

ME?" cried Winston, "FLY?"

"Yes," said Eduardo as if it was a perfectly ordinary everyday thing for a mouse to take to the skies. "It'll be easy! Look—there's a Winston-sized seat behind the controls of that plane. We'll take it up to the roof and you can set off from there. You'll be at the North Pole in no time at all—you might even meet Santa Claus's sleigh on the way!"

Winston wasn't sure about Eduardo's idea. It was dangerous enough for a little mouse like him just walking about the city; he didn't dare to imagine what it might be like to fly above one! And how would he ever know which way the North Pole was? He didn't have a map.

"Don't worry!" said Eduardo, as if reading Winston's mind. "Look for the brightest star in the sky and that's the North Star. Just follow that and you'll know you are going the right way."

Winston still wasn't convinced, but then he looked at the envelope he'd been carrying all evening. *Everyone deserves a merry Christmas,* he thought to himself.

He HAD to fly that plane to the North Pole and complete his mission—no matter how scary it was. He stuck out his chin and nodded.

"I'll do it!" he said.

"OH BRAVO!" hooted Eduardo, beaming. "We haven't a moment to lose!"

They clambered up the mechanical Santa Claus and, standing on his head, unhooked the toy plane from the ceiling and carefully lowered it to the ground.

"Okay!" Eduardo puffed, when they were safely back on the floor. "Now we just need to get it up to the roof."

Winston thought of all the hundreds of steps that wound up and around the five stories from the entrance hall and he groaned. "It's going to take us all night to get up the stairs with this! It's really heavy."

"Oh, we aren't going to take the stairs. We'll whizz up to the roof in the elevator!" said Eduardo. "Follow me!"

Winston hadn't a clue what an elevator was, but he had no choice other than to help Eduardo with the plane and tag along with him. He walked as briskly as he could toward a row of shiny brass doors set in a row on a nearby wall. Potted palm plants separated them, and Eduardo scampered up one to press a little button on the wall.

The ground immediately began to tremble and Winston felt afraid. What was happening? He glanced at Eduardo. He was back beside

Winston now and was cheerfully waiting and whistling a jolly Christmas tune.

The trembling stopped and one set of doors opened, revealing a velvet-lined and gold-trimmed elevator. Eduardo hurried Winston and the plane inside. He clambered up the velvet wall coverings and pressed a little button that was hidden behind a small plate underneath rows of other larger buttons. The entire thing started to shake and shudder as it began to whoosh upward.

"That's a secret button for getting straight to the roof," said Eduardo proudly. "Only important staff like me know about it . . ."

Winston would never forget the short journey in the elevator. He didn't know what was up or down, he was jostled all about and he tumbled over several times. It was a relief when they came to a stop and the doors flew open with a little ding of a bell.

They dragged the plane out onto the roof and looked around in silence. The weather had taken a turn for the worse while Winston had been inside the department store. A fearful wind roared and howled and thick curtains of snow swirled around him making it very difficult to see.

Winston gulped. His fur was prickling with nerves. If he squinted, he could just make out the other buildings of the city stretching out all around him. He was very high up and he could hear the traffic purring far below.

"We'll need a good runway for you to take off from!" shouted Eduardo over the wind. He pointed to a raised buttress at the back of the building. It was only a foot or so off the ground and by pushing and shoving and heaving and pulling they got the plane up on top of it.

The tiny plane rocked wildly. The propeller started to spin. Winston clambered into the cockpit. There was another seat behind him, but it was too small for Eduardo to join him.

"You'll have to stay here!" shouted Winston over the noise. "Thank you for all your help!"

Eduardo patted Winston kindly on the paw. "You are welcome here at Fortesque's any time you like!"

Winston nestled down into his seat and gripped the controls tightly. Eduardo started to push the plane, slowly at first, and then faster and faster. The edge of the building came into view, and beyond it just seemed like a big black void with snow swirling like a whirlpool.

The propellor whirred.

Winston held his breath.

And with a final shove, Eduardo pushed Winston and the plane over the edge of the roof.

MAKE A SNOW GLOBE

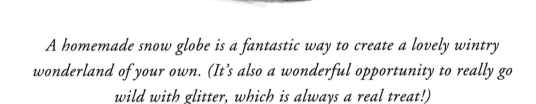

A homemade snow globe is a fantastic way to create a lovely wintry wonderland of your own. (It's also a wonderful opportunity to really go wild with glitter, which is always a real treat!)

YOU WILL NEED:

A SCREW-TOP JAR
A SMALL PLASTIC TOY—YOU COULD USE SOME
CHRISTMAS CAKE DECORATIONS
GLYCERINE—YOU CAN FIND THIS IN THE BAKING AISLE
GLUE—NOT WATER-SOLUBLE
GLITTER

Don't worry if you don't have any glycerine. It does make the glitter float better but it's not essential!

1. Fill your jar with water and screw the lid on.

2. Shake it about to make sure there aren't any leaks.

3. Take the lid off and dry it with a dish towel. Then glue your toy to the inside of the lid. Leave it to dry for twenty minutes.

4. Empty the jar and re-fill it using two parts water and one part glycerine. The glycerine thickens the water so that your glitter snow will fall slowly.

5. Sprinkle in the glitter and give it a good stir.

6. Screw the lid back on VERY tightly.

Now get shaking!

A LIGHT IN THE SKY

He was actually flying! He quickly discovered that it was quite difficult to keep the plane going in the right direction. The wind really was dreadfully fierce and snow whirled around so that he could barely see the front of the little aircraft.

"Follow the brightest star in the sky!" Winston told himself, remembering Eduardo's words.

But it was quite difficult to even know where the sky was! The snowstorm became a full-blown blizzard and the plane was buffeted in all directions.

Winston shivered and concentrated on trying to keep hold of the letter. He kept looking for any flashes of bright light that could be the North Star.

As he was pulling the plane up out of a sharp dive, he spotted a light in the sky. He blinked and tried to find it again.

Aha! There it was! It was some way off in the distance. A little bright red circle of light. What could that possibly be? Winston banked to the left, toward the strange glowing orb, but it disappeared into the thick white fog of the blizzard.

"Oh, great cheese and crackers!" exclaimed Winston.

All of a sudden, the red glowing light was almost on top of him. He was heading straight for it! It was too late to avoid a collision! Winston grabbed hold of the letter with both paws and crouched as low as he could in his seat. A confusion of fur and legs and antlers raced toward him. He closed his eyes tight.

The plane's tiny propellers snapped off and a wing was almost completely torn away. It spiraled downward faster and faster. The wind whistled past Winston's ears and he carefully opened his eyes. Dark shapes were speeding toward him. Buildings, he realized. Big ones. He was still above the city. The large, wide roof of a skyscraper was rushing toward him. Suddenly, Winston was thrown clear from the plane and found himself falling through the night sky before landing with a wallop in a deep snowdrift on the roof of a tall building.

The last thing Winston heard before everything went cold and white was the sound of the tiny toy plane crashing and splintering into pieces.

MAKE CHRISTMAS TABLE DECORATIONS

Decorating your table for Christmas is a wonderful way to make it look pretty—especially if you have visitors coming for dinner. There are a lot of things you can do: make party hats, write a fancy menu, or make place cards for your family.

YOU WILL NEED:

A GLASS BOWL OR VASE

PINECONES AND NUTS IN THEIR SHELLS

ORNAMENTS

A ROLL OF BROWN PAPER AND SOME COLORED PENCILS

TEA LIGHTS AND FLOATING CANDLES

HOLLY

1. Making a Christmas centerpiece for your table is really easy and there are lots of variations you can try! Find a medium-sized glass bowl or vase (make sure a grown-up says you can use it!) and fill it with Christmassy knick-knacks. You can use Christmas ornaments, pine cones, nuts in their shells, and even holly.

2. You can also try filling a flat dish with water and putting some floating tea lights in. Try putting some marbles and whole cranberries in the bowl below the tea lights. This will look really nice and you will have your very own Christmas bowl! Ask a grown-up to light the candles for you and enjoy the gorgeous centerpiece you have just made.

3. Instead of a tablecloth, make a table runner using a roll of brown paper—roll it down the center of the table on top of the tablecloth before you lay the table. Give everyone some pencils or crayons and they can decorate it when they have finished their meal.

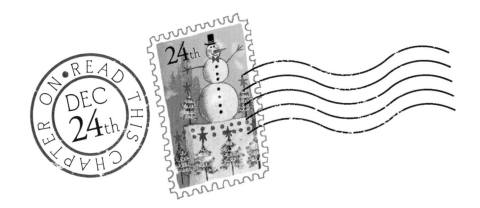

THE END

All was white and silent.

Minutes ticked by. Eventually Winston managed to open his eyes and a great buzzing and ringing sounded in his ears. He crawled out from under the snow. Winston had no idea where he was or even how far he'd traveled from Fortesque's.

"What am I going to do now?" he whispered to himself.

Everything seemed hopeless: the letter, Christmas, finding somewhere safe and warm for himself out of the storm. He stood as best he could in the wind and looked all around. He felt utterly lost and completely alone.

Across the great expanse of the rooftop where he had crash-landed, someone was moving about. He glimpsed a blur of red. He realized that this could be his only hope of getting down from this roof to safety. The snow whirled, and the figure disappeared into the whiteness. *Where did it go?* Winston wondered. He was so tired and achy now, he could barely stand. The figure in red swam into view. He looked again, trying to make out what it was. He gasped. It couldn't be!

"Wait!" cried Winston. "WAIT!"

But his squeaks were snatched away by the wind.

He'd have to run he thought, so he pitter-pattered across the roof as fast as his tiny feet could carry him waving the envelope above his head.

The snow was coming thick and fast, the wind was howling, and everything was white and confusing. It was like being in a snow globe that was being madly shaken about.

"Wait!" Winston squeaked again. He couldn't walk another step. A blast of wind knocked him over and he landed on top of the envelope with a bump. He was too exhausted to get up again, so he just lay there shivering . . .

✳

A few moments later, the figure appeared again out of the whiteness. He was small and round with a fluffy white beard and rosy red cheeks peeking out like two cherries on top of an ice cream. He was bundled up against the chill in a cheerful outfit. Winston opened one eye as wide as he could manage and smiled weakly.

"I knew I'd find you!" he squeaked.

Santa Claus cocked an ear. What was that? He'd heard a noise.

It was a tiny and squeaky sort of a noise, but he'd definitely heard it. It sounded like a mouse. But what on earth would a mouse being doing up on a roof in this awful weather?

He looked around him and spotted what looked like the broken remains of a toy plane sticking out of a snow drift. Then he spotted something else. Lying on the ground almost completely covered in snow was the tiniest mouse he'd ever seen. And he seemed to be holding on to something very tightly.

Santa Claus gently picked Winston up and carefully placed him in his pocket for warmth. Then he looked with interest at the damp and crumpled piece of paper the little creature had been holding.

It was an envelope. And it was addressed to him! And inside, a letter from Oliver—the little boy who lives above the toy shop on Mistletoe Street.

Santa Claus scratched his head for a moment. He hadn't heard from Oliver this year. He'd thought maybe the boy had grown too old and had stopped believing. But now he had his letter in his hand. Had it got lost in the mail? Could that tiny little creature have been trying to deliver it? Surely not on a fearful night like this? It seemed unbelievable, yet here was a mouse on the roof holding the letter in his little paws.

"Extraordinary!" said Santa Claus, shaking his head in amazement.

He tucked Oliver's letter into his jacket for safety and carefully reached into his pocket. Winston had found a spare glove in there and had curled up inside it to keep warm so Santa Claus picked him up—glove and all—and looked at him.

"And what about you?" he said quietly, as he stroked Winston's head. "What would a brave little thing like you wish for at Christmas?"

Winston didn't say anything. He was fast asleep. He just snuggled deeper into his warm makeshift sleeping bag and snored loudly.

"I see . . ." said Santa Claus, and his eyes twinkled magically.

He looked up at the sky. The wind had stopped howling and the blizzard had calmed, so the snow was once again falling lazily on the city.

"I think I've got one extra little delivery to make before morning," he said.

And he put Winston carefully back in his pocket, climbed into his sleigh and, with a flick of the reins, took off over the rooftops and up into the sky.

CHRISTMAS CHECKLIST

Use this Christmas checklist to make sure you have done everything you needed to before Christmas Day! Christmas can be a very busy time, so it will help to stay organized if you can.

✶ Write a letter to Santa Claus.

✶ Gifts—have you bought all the gifts you need? Are they all wrapped and labeled?

✶ Decorate your tree—Christmas isn't complete without decorating a tree! Make sure you help a grown-up decorate the Christmas tree as soon as it goes up.

✶ Decorate the house.

✶ Read a Christmas book.

✶ Sing a Christmas song.

✶ Bake Christmas food.

✶ Watch a Christmas film.

✶ Play games with your family.

✶ Go for a walk.

✶ Write Christmas cards to your friends and family. It's also nice to write a card to your teacher.

✶ Tell some Christmas jokes.

✶ Christmas Eve—put your stocking by the fireplace and leave out some cookies and milk for Santa. He has a very long way to go tonight so he needs to be well fed! Be sure to also leave out some carrots for Rudolf and all the other reindeer.

HOT BUTTERED TOAST

Even before he'd opened his eyes, Winston knew that something very strange and unusual had happened. The last thing he could remember was being outside in the freezing cold with the angry wind and snow roaring all around him. And he remembered being tired. Very tired indeed and freezing cold too—the sort of cold that makes you feel frozen from the inside out.

But that wasn't the case now at all. Winston was—he considered it for a moment—he was SNUGGLY. Really warm and cozy and, yes, very snuggly indeed. He sniffed. His whiskers wobbled with excitement. What was that lovely smell? It smelled like someone nearby was cooking something very delicious. Where on earth was he?

He opened his eyes and looked around him and gasped. What had happened? He wasn't outside on the street in a hidey-hole, which was where he woke up most mornings. He was in a bed! A perfect little mouse-sized bed with soft flannel sheets, a thick blanket, and two great big plump pillows. There was even a little patchwork quilt keeping him warm.

Winston wiggled his toes and looked around. He seemed to be in a little bedroom in a house where everything was just the right size for him. There were tiny books, a small armchair and—as Winston peeked over to look down the side of his bed—on the floor was a pair of tiny slippers which Winston knew, just from looking at them, would fit his feet perfectly.

What is this lovely place? he wondered.

A house made just for a mouse? Was he still asleep? Was he dreaming?

Then he heard a noise. A great stampede of thuds and whoops—of footsteps and voices. Human voices.

"Now be careful on the stairs, Oliver! What on earth has got you so giddy this morning?"

There were some very excited squeaking noises before Winston heard:

"What letter, Oliver?"

Oliver? thought Winston. *Who was Oliver?*

Just then there was a rattling noise. It sounded like someone was right outside his room. Winston burrowed down deep beneath his bed covers so only his eyes were peeking out over the top of his blanket.

He couldn't believe what he was seeing! The entire far wall of his room swung open and a little boy's face appeared.

The little boy was in his pajamas and his curly hair was sticking wildly up on end. His cheeks were bright pink and his eyes were sparkling with excitement.

"Mom! Dad!" he cried. "Come and see! In the doll's house—there's a mouse! A real mouse fast asleep in the attic!"

There followed a great commotion as more faces joined the little boy's to peer in at Winston. Two were grown-up faces, and the other was a smaller face. All belonged to humans in pajamas and nightgowns and everyone looked like they had jumped out of bed in a great hurry!

"Goodness!" said a grown-up face with the bristly moustache under its nose. "There IS a mouse in the doll's house!"

"Santa Claus said in his letter that I would find a friend in the doll's house! And it's a mouse!" squeaked the little boy.

"What letter, Oliver?" said the other grown-up face. This one didn't have a moustache, but had its hair up in a headscarf.

The other very small face didn't say anything. She was too busy sucking on the sleeve of her nightie.

The little boy quickly handed over a small sheet of paper. "This letter!" he said, shivering with excitement. "It's from Santa Claus! I found it in my stocking this morning—look!"

The two grown-ups read the letter and as they did their eyes grew bigger and bigger with astonishment.

Dear Oliver,

Thank you for your letter. I believe it had rather an exciting journey to get to me, but the important thing is that it found me in the end.

I understand from your note that what you would like more than anything this Christmas is a friend—someone to go on adventures with.

If you go downstairs and peek in at the attic bedroom of that lovely doll's house you will find a little someone there waiting for you. He should be a very suitable friend for you. (He's really good at adventuring!) I should think he'll be fast asleep when you find him. He's had quite a tiring evening.

Take great care of each other. I look forward to reading about all your adventures together in your letter next Christmas. Although maybe pop it in the mail a little earlier next year!

Merry Christmas
Your friend,
Santa Claus

"Well I never, Oliver!" exclaimed the grown-up with the headscarf. "A mouse!"

The little boy beamed.

"I think we'd all better go and get dressed and then our new friend here can join us in the kitchen for breakfast!" said the grown-up with the moustache. "Do you think he'd like some hot buttered toast?"

"He does look like he could do with a good meal," said the other grown-up, smiling.

Oliver told his new friend that he'd be back for him as soon as he

was dressed (and had brushed his hair, one of the grown-ups added) and the whole family scampered off to get ready for the day.

When he was alone, Winston sat up and blinked. He wasn't a street mouse any more. He had a warm home and—if the lovely smells were to be believed—a yummy breakfast, lunch, and dinner ahead of him. He also had a friend named Oliver. How extraordinary!

Something crinkled at the foot of his bed and Winston scrambled about in the blankets until he found what it was: a stocking! A little mouse-sized striped stocking and in it was a tiny letter written in the smallest mouse-sized writing he'd ever seen.

Dear Winston,

Thank you so much for delivering Oliver's letter to me.

I can only imagine what sort of an evening you had trying to deliver it. It must have been very exciting, but dangerous, too.

What a kind and brave mouse you are. For such a tiny creature you have an enormous heart: one which understands that nobody should ever be left out or forgotten—especially at Christmas.

Merry Christmas, Winston. And enjoy your new home.

With love from
Santa Claus

Winston folded the letter carefully and held it very close to his chest. Then he snuggled back down under the blankets in his new bed in his new house in his new home and for the first time in his life he felt warm from the tip of his nose to the end of his tail.

And as he lay there he wondered what adventures tomorrow would bring.

The End

Until next Christmas . . .

TIPS FOR NEXT YEAR

✱ Keep old Christmas cards: when Christmas is finished, ask if you can have some of the old Christmas cards. There are tons of great things you can make from them—just save and store them away for next Christmas!

✱ Collect cardboard boxes in all shapes and sizes! You can wrap these in wrapping paper and make larger Christmas boxes.

✱ Collect any ribbons you come across. These are great for wrapping and hanging homemade decorations.

✱ Keep a note of any fun games you play throughout the year. Christmas is a great time to play games with family and friends, and they'll love any new suggestions you might have.

✱ Listen to people. If you listen carefully to what your friends and family are saying throughout the year, you will have a great idea of what to buy them or make them next year for Christmas. You can show them that you are really thoughtful this way.

✱ Don't throw away any old toys you don't want. Keep them in a safe place and then ask a grown-up if you can donate them to a children's charity at Christmas next year—everyone needs an extra bit of love and care at Christmas!

WE WISH YOU A MERRY CHRISTMAS

We wish you a merry Christmas
We wish you a merry Christmas
We wish you a merry Christmas
And a happy New Year.

Good tidings we bring
to you and your kin.
We wish you a merry Christmas
And a happy New Year.

Now bring us some figgy pudding
Now bring us some figgy pudding
Now bring us some figgy pudding
And bring some out here.

Chorus

For we all like figgy pudding
For we all like figgy pudding
For we all like figgy pudding
So bring some out here.

Chorus

And we won't go until we've had some
And we won't go until we've had some
And we won't go until we've had some
So bring some out here.

Chorus

'TWAS THE NIGHT BEFORE CHRISTMAS

'Twas the night before Christmas, when all through the house
Not a creature was stirring, not even a mouse;
The stockings were hung by the chimney with care,
In hopes that St. Nicholas soon would be there;
The children were nestled all snug in their beds,
While visions of sugarplums danced in their heads;
And mamma in her 'kerchief, and I in my cap,
Had just settled our brains for a long winter's nap,
When out on the lawn there arose such a clatter,
I sprang from my bed to see what was the matter.
Away to the window I flew like a flash,
Tore open the shutters, and threw up the sash.
The moon, on the breast of the new-fallen snow
Gave the luster of midday to objects below,
When, what to my wondering eyes should appear,
But a miniature sleigh and eight tiny reindeer,
With a little old driver, so lively and quick,
I knew in a moment it must be St. Nick.
More rapid than eagles his coursers they came,
And he whistled, and shouted, and called them by name:
"Now, Dasher! Now, Dancer! Now, Prancer and Vixen!
On, Comet! On, Cupid! On, Donder and Blitzen!
To the top of the porch! To the top of the wall!
Now dash away! Dash away! Dash away all!"
As dry leaves that before the wild hurricane fly,
When they meet with an obstacles, mount to the sky,

So up to the housetop the coursers they flew,
With the sleigh full of toys, and St. Nicholas too.
And then, in a twinkling, I heard on the roof
The prancing and pawing of each little hoof.
As I drew in my head, and was turning around,
Down the chimney St. Nicholas came with a bound.
He was dressed all in fur, from his head to his foot,
And his clothes were all tarnished with ashes and soot;
A bundle of toys he had flung on his back,
And he looked like a pedlar just opening his pack.
His eyes—how they twinkled; his dimples, how merry!
His cheeks were like roses, his nose like a cherry!
His droll little mouth was drawn up like a bow,
And the beard of his chin was as white as the snow;
The stump of a pipe he held tight in his teeth,
And the smoke it encircled his head like a wreath;
He had a broad face and a little round belly,
That shook, when he laughed, like a bowlful of jelly.
He was chubby and plump, a right jolly old elf,
And I laughed when I saw him, in spite of myself;
A wink of his eye and a twist of his head,
Soon gave me to know I had nothing to dread;
He spoke not a word, but went straight to his work,
And filled all the stockings; then turned with a jerk,
And laying his finger aside of his nose,
And giving a nod, up the chimney he rose;
He sprang to his sleigh, to his team gave a whistle,
And away they all flew like the down of a thistle.
But I heard him exclaim, 'ere he drove out of sight,
"Merry Christmas to all, and to all a good night!"

CLEMENT CLARKE MOORE

JINGLE BELLS

Dashing through the snow,
In a one-horse open sleigh;
O'er the fields we go,
Laughing all the way;
Bells on bob-tail ring,
Making spirits bright;
Oh what fun to ride and sing
A sleighing song tonight.

Jingle bells, jingle bells,
Jingle all the way;
Oh! What joy it is to ride
In a one-horse open sleigh.
Jingle bells, jingle bells,
Jingle all the way;
Oh! What a joy it is to ride
In a one-horse open sleigh.

JAMES PIERPOINT

THE TWELVE DAYS OF CHRISTMAS

On the first day of Christmas
My true love sent to me
A partridge in a pear tree.

On the second day of Christmas
My true love sent to me
Two turtle doves
And a partridge in a pear tree.

On the third day of Christmas
My true love sent to me
Three French hens, two turtle doves,
And a partridge in a pear tree.

On the fourth day of Christmas
My true love sent to me
Four calling birds, three French hens,
Two turtle doves, and a partridge in a pear tree.

On the fifth day of Christmas
my true love sent to me
Five golden rings, four calling birds,
three French hens, two turtle doves,
and a partridge in a pear tree

On the sixth day of Christmas
My true love sent to me
Six geese a-laying, five golden rings,
Four calling birds, three French hens,
Two turtle doves, and a partridge in a pear tree.

On the seventh day of Christmas
My true love sent to me
Seven swans a-swimming,
Six geese a-laying, etc.

On the eighth day of Christmas
My true love sent to me,
Eight maids a-milking,
Seven swans a-swimming, etc.

On the ninth day of Christmas
My true love sent to me
Nine drummers drumming,
Eight maids a-milking, etc.

On the tenth day of Christmas
My true love sent to me
Ten pipers piping,
Nine drummers drumming, etc.

On the eleventh day of Christmas
My true love sent to me
Eleven ladies dancing,
Ten pipers piping, etc.

On the twelfth day of Christmas
My true love sent to me
Twelve lords a-leaping,
Eleven ladies dancing,
Ten pipers piping,
Nine drummers drumming,
Eight maids a-milking,
Seven swans a-swimming,
Six geese a-laying,
Five gold rings,
Four calling birds,
Three French hens,
Two turtle doves,
And a partridge in a pear tree.

ANON

Hello!

I've always loved winter. All those frosty mornings and getting cozy after being outside in the cold. And when December arrives, Christmas magic is in the air!

The bustling shops, the glitzy decorations, the waiting, and then of course, the big day itself!

I got the idea for this book when I was helping my niece and nephews write their letters to Santa Claus and I wondered (with a shiver) what would happen if one of the letters got lost? Hopefully there would be some kind person (or in this case a mouse) to deliver it for us. And what adventures would they have?

A Christmas angel I made aged 4! (He's very old now!)

Of course Christmas isn't just about the things you buy from the shops. I wanted to write a story about the sorts of things that are free—like bravery and kindness. I hope Winston's Christmas adventure shows you that you are never too tiny to be brave and that little acts of kindness can often make huge differences to other people.

I hope you've enjoyed this book and that you might come back to it next year and share it with other people in your family and with friends.

Have a very cozy Christmas and an adventurous New Year!

love from Alex
x

Me, aged two, playing in the snow!